THE PHANTOM CIRCUIT

AUSTIN FARMER

THE
PHANTOM
CIRCUIT

CHAPTER ONE

For years, I prepared myself to hear the worst. I imagined every possibility about the very moment I would receive the news—where I would be, who I would be with, how I would feel. I felt guilty for thinking about death and the afterlife so often. It scared me, because nobody really knew. In the end, it didn't make it any easier.

Dianne was gone.

I was heartbroken. And then I became numb, vulnerable to the invisible, malevolent forces surrounding me. I used social media as a way to connect, to forget. Some nights, I experienced an underwater sensation, as though watching the world from below, distant and kaleidoscopic. I was sinking behind the horizon, waiting for somebody to pull me through to the other side.

On my timeline, people were having kids. Friends of friends were dying. Old high school classmates were buying their first houses. Celebratory posts and obituary posts scrolled by. It was almost impossible for me to comprehend the pandemic.

Meanwhile, I was broke. There was so much happening in the world, and yet, it was hard enough to process the things happening within my own world, my own timeline. I hadn't posted on my rideshare blog for about a year before things shut down. I tried to update my profile, but I didn't know what to say. Now, I couldn't say anything. I couldn't even look at my screen.

Healing is never linear. I kept reminding myself that. Though I compartmentalized my life into different moments, chapters, and memories, it was truly difficult to cherish the good ones when I didn't even want to think about her. I couldn't intervene again. Two interventions were already too many. I needed to pull myself out of this limbo. I needed to learn how to accept the things I couldn't control. Sometimes, it felt as though I was thrown into a world full of ghosts, and I had no choice but to hide from them.

I tried expressing these things to Mom on our Facetime call as I sat alone in a Carl's Junior parking lot, waiting for my next passenger to pop up in the Lyft app. Sometimes the waiting period between passengers could take an hour, if I was lucky enough to get a passenger at all. Nobody was going out. I didn't even want to drive, but I had to make some money before unemployment kicked in.

"Are you alright, sweetheart?" Mom's voice was comforting in the dead silence outside. In my rearview mirror, a broken streetlight strobed on and off, creating weird fractals of a broken world I wished to run from. I tried not to look into the mirror lately. Only when I had to.

"I'm not sure, Mom. I honestly don't know how to answer that."

"Is it something else?"

I nodded. "Kind of."

I took a deep breath, shook my head, and tried to smile. I liked to pretend that things weren't as bad as they were, but my imagination only went so far. I could see Mom's instant frown. She knew what I was thinking, and I didn't have to say anything, really, because she already knew. On Facetime, I couldn't hide anything. I hated looking at myself in the screen. My mind played tricks on me. I looked like someone else.

"She's not your responsibility, Erica."

"Yeah, I know. But last night, she sent me these messages—"

"She's not supposed to text you. Did you do what we talked about?"

"Yes. And, no. I couldn't help it, Mom. I didn't mean to read them. But I couldn't *not* read them. I tried to watch TV after I came home but I kept rereading them because they were right there in front of me."

"It's okay. It doesn't matter what she said."

"But it seemed different, Mom. This time, something's really wrong. I'm scared. I'm sorry."

I fought back tears. I had already cried myself to sleep many nights when I found out that I had lost all of my gigs. I felt melodramatic, sensitive, and slightly out of control. But I guess that was just a natural response to everything happening in the world. I didn't have the strength to cry again.

Outside, the bells of San Diego's trolley echoed throughout the streets. I jumped, half expecting to see Dianne in the mirror. I was definitely losing it and I needed my sister to comfort me.

"Sorry, for what?"

"Because I keep making things worse. Like those times when I saw her when I wasn't supposed to, and she looked different. I could barely recognize her. She barely remembered my name."

"We've already been through this many times with her. If she needs to come back home, she will come back to our place, and hopefully this time, she'll stay. Have you been talking with your friends? Have you asked to schedule some fun Zoom calls? Maybe that'll help to take your mind off things."

"A few. I don't know, Mom. Everyone's in their own bubbles right now. I don't want to bother them. Sometimes it feels like I have no one. I know that's not true but it feels that way a lot of times. I just don't know what to think anymore."

"You've been so strong throughout all of this. I'm so proud of you, Erica. This will all come to pass. You have to focus on yourself now. You can't let Dianne stop you from living your life, okay? Do what you need to do to get through this and call me anytime."

"I know. Thanks, Mom." A notification popped up on my phone. A passenger had requested a ride. "I don't know how much longer I can keep doing this. I have to go. I love you."

As I turned on my car, I couldn't help but notice something strange moving in the rearview mirror again, something that was not of this world. A brief pulse of light flashed across the glass, as though somewhere deep within the universe, a star had just imploded, and its fragments were being pulled into the void beyond.

~ ~ ~

I was driving on the Interstate 5, finishing up my last ride, when I heard my passenger casually mention that the police had found Dianne's body.

I lost my grip on the wheel and tapped the breaks. The car stuttered and swerved, the front wheels skidding across the fast lane to the center divider, scraping across the cement wall. Sparks erupted in volcanic tornadoes. The sharp scent of grating metal and burning rubber swept through the vents.

"Miss, are you all right?"

I caught my breath, grasping for ten and two on the wheel, and then four and eight, seven and twelve, steadying my shaking wrists. Trying my best to refocus on switching lanes, I managed to stabilize the car before we spun out.

"Did you say *Dianne Westfield?*"

"Yeah." My passenger buckled his seatbelt a little tighter. He was a sixty-something inebriated businessman rushing home after his luxurious business conference had been suddenly cancelled due to the pandemic. If he weren't already drunk, he probably would have cancelled my ride, told me to pull over, and threatened me with a one-star rating. "It's Dianne Westfield, all right. The girl from that singing competition show. The international superstar. It's all over my timeline. Are you a fan of hers or something?"

"Something like that…" My voice trailed off as I checked the speedometer. I was nearing 85 mph. Through the windshield, the world spun around me. I eased off the gas and coasted until I hit 65, fooling everyone driving next to me that I was okay, really, I was *fine*, not having a panic attack.

"To be honest, Miss Erica, doesn't quite look like it. Oh, I know! You were her biggest fan, am I right? I could tell. I mean, who wouldn't be a fan of *Dianne*! Is that it?"

I glanced at the GPS. We were approximately one mile away from the drop-off destination. The blue arrow avatar that represented my car was flashing, alerting me in a strobing, red exclamation mark that I needed to slow the heck down. I needed to remain calm. Sane. Professional.

Looking in the rearview mirror, I checked my surroundings, trying my best to ground myself. I remembered how I had played Bloody Mary with Dianne one night. It was always on my mind, really. It had been the most terrifying moment of my life. I had seen my life flash before my eyes. I had stood there, entranced, staring into the mirror, watching my future unfold as the looking glass surrounded me, helpless to its trajectory, capable of distorting the past and the faces within.

At the other end of the mirror, I had seen Dianne.

She was floating there, sinking into a starless void. From the other side, she had spoken to me, asking for someone to pull her through the shadows. I reached out to her, but her hands only went through mine. She had become an outline of her former self, then, distorted starlight wavering through her skin, revealing the stars and the emptiness beyond. A ghost. Like she was now.

Why would the stars eat her up? I had asked myself then.

Now, I felt that terror creeping back in. What if she was still in that same mirror, caught in Bloody Mary's grasp? She was somewhere else now. Maybe even right in front of me. I needed to know where.

"Why're you so quiet?" asked my passenger.

"Please, stop."

"Stop what?"

"*Sir.*"

"Tell me if I offended you." He took off his seatbelt, slid to the middle seat, and leaned in. His breath reeked of whiskey. "Tell me."

"Sir, please keep your seatbelt buckled at all times." It was all I could do. I had to keep my eyes on the road ahead, no matter what. "And please keep your mask on."

"The fame must've been too much for her sweet little head. All the attention. Would make anyone a druggie. Must've been crazy-making."

"Please *shut the hell up*!"

I pulled up to his destination, a lonely motel on the outskirts of Old Town, San Diego. I coasted, flashed my hazards, and put the car in park.

"Lady, you're the worst driver I've ever had."

"Told you to buckle your seatbelt, *you jerk.*"

I let him curse me out as he threatened to call Lyft headquarters. He stumbled out of the car and was barely able to close the door behind him. I followed his reflection in the rearview mirror until it became eclipsed by a shadow. Odd, since there wasn't anything casting that light. For a moment, it seemed as though something else was trying to see through the other side of the mirror. Bloody Mary, maybe. Or Dianne, floating through that starless void, reaching through the shadows, calling to me.

As he disappeared into the darkness, I parked the car. Then I turned off the app and wept.

When you look in the mirror, how can you be so sure who's staring back?

CHAPTER TWO

My body grew hollow.

It was as though someone had carved out my core, removing my warmth like a jack-o-lantern stripped of its candle. I had experienced depression before, but nothing quite like this. It crept instantly through me, a thick sludge pumping through my veins. It fossilized and pressed its weight against my chest. Once I got back to my apartment, a compulsion overcame me to sit and do nothing.

I opened my laptop and pulled up Facebook. I didn't post about it online, not at first. Everyone else was already doing that. I didn't even have a chance to catch up. My inbox was inundated with strangers. I read as many messages as I could and left them on **SEEN**, not because I didn't appreciate them, but because they felt like they were meant for someone else.

My timeline was filled with avatars grieving for Dianne.

It was a ghost town, really. I didn't know at least half of these people anymore. Nobody referred to what had actually happened, how she'd died, because nobody really knew what to say. It put me into some bizarre, surreal state. Sure, everybody had good intentions, but it was all so overwhelming. The pandemic was enough to begin with. Did everyone expect me to respond to every single message? There was no way these people really cared as much as they put off. Why would somebody from my second-grade class—someone I hadn't spoken to for over two decades—all of a sudden pretend to know the recently famous Dianne?

Hindsight is a kind of superpower.

You can perceive time, and your relationships, in a special way. Being alive not only meant that I possessed memories, but also I could *relive* them, too. I could be in two places at once—the past and the present, living among ghosts.

It was a bad time to live alone. My mind swept to dark places, brimming with thoughts I reckoned people would shudder at if they knew what I was thinking. My profile picture displayed someone who looked happy, but I couldn't even remember the last time I had taken a smiling selfie in real life. If the computer monitor was a mirror, too, then there was something within it that knew the truth, something that could see through the looking glass and straight into my soul. Perhaps it was an algorithm, deeply embedded in my profile, making it increasingly more difficult to post anything at all. Or maybe it wasn't something, but someone, who had been there all along.

It was Bloody Mary, waiting to pull me back through to the other side of her mirror.

I needed to sleep and find a way to crawl out of this black hole. But before that, I needed to post something, anything, so people wouldn't start to worry about me.

I scrolled my mouse over to the status update. **WHAT'S ON YOUR MIND, ERICA?**

I stared into the void. It stared back at me.

I started typing something. It didn't feel quite right. I deleted what I wrote and typed again. I felt like I was writing a get-well-soon card to someone I didn't know. I entered Hallmark-Land in my head. It was sort of manic, I guess. The doors were always open if you knew how to get there. All you had to do was put the words in the right order, unlocking the secret door at the end of the hallway in your mind, where the words were always hovering on the edges of comprehension. Everything I wrote felt disposable. I was in a thrift store of discarded cards, faded glitter pouring through their spines, scratch-and-sniff stickers plastered across their bodies.

It was kind of funny, seeing myself in the laptop screen writing the words in real time. I was laughing, deleting them, shaking my head, nodding in agreement, as I hid behind my profile, pixels bursting through my fingertips. The tip of my tongue danced with possibilities. Finally, a sentence floated to the forefront of my mind, almost as though the words were already written.

I wish I could see you again, Dianne, the real you.

And then I clicked **ENTER**.

Because it was true. So true. As much as I'd grown to hate her, I hated her because I loved her. But she had become somebody else.

I waited.

The edge of my mouth lifted into a smile as the *likes* started pouring in. Every notification made my body buzz. Maybe I was experiencing what she felt like when she was high, strolling through fast food drive-thrus, begging for money, living off protein bars and prayers. She was my blood and it ran in my blood, too, this thing that possessed her and controlled her and became her.

The computer speakers chimed.

I couldn't stop staring at myself in the computer screen. I licked the corners of my lips in an inevitable Pavlovian fashion. The metallic flavor on my tongue reminded me of a taste I encountered once in a dream where I met God, or the outline of it, a face shining through the fog. Maybe that omniscient being was lying dormant, waiting for the right moment to intervene.

I had tried intervening. Interventions didn't work, unless they *did*.

I stared at myself for so long that I started to look like a stranger. A reflection is like a memory. The person you see is a person who existed a moment ago. In my reflection, my eyes started blending in with the pixels. It was only a moment, but it was all I needed to know something was wrong.

I shouldn't have posted anything.

I should have waited. But for what?

I was about to delete my post when something popped up on my screen.

A notification. A new message, in my inbox.

I hovered the mouse over the **MESSENGER** cloud icon.

Part of me already knew who it was from. I should have just gone to sleep and never checked my messages ever again.

It was from Dianne.

CHAPTER THREE

It was just one word, but I couldn't look away.

Dianne: *Hey.*

My stomach dropped. Why would someone make a mockery of Dianne's death? I took a deep breath and had to remind myself that these were only pixels. These were merely thumbs, fingers dancing across a keyboard behind a screen, which someone was clearly hiding behind. At least, that's what I kept telling myself.

Obviously, this was just a hacker trying to screw with me. Many people had created imposter accounts for Dianne after she won *Anthem* Season 1. The weird thing was, this was from her real account, the one I'd blocked a while back. I had never seen such an immediate turnaround for something like this. All I could do was stare at it, the way the letters looked on the screen, the tail of the *y* dancing between the syllable *eeeyyyy*, waltzing across the screen, a welcome invitation to respond.

A gush of hysterical laughter sprang from my chest like a jack-in-the-box. My brain filled with sparkles of responses, the words elongating like slinkies. Each message stretched, falling down an ascending staircase, eternally propelled into the future.

What was I supposed to say? *Hey, Dianne, so good to see you?* Yeah, right. What was "she" going to say? "Hey" back?

I couldn't leave her on ·**READ** again. Not after last night. I had failed her. But this wasn't her. I'd heard of fake funeral homes conning people before. Now, it was actually happening to me. So, I had to respond with something.

Erica: *Dianne?*

My eyes stung. I refused to cry again. I don't know why I stayed up to read the response. Maybe because part of me wanted to believe it was actually her. I was already gravitating toward the realm of emotions beyond shock, so even if I knew it wasn't her, a sliver of me clung to the idea it *could be* her.

The screen filled with an ellipses, those three dots that caused so much turmoil in so many millennials. Someone was typing, but who?

Dianne: *There's no time for questions.*

Erica: *Of course there is. I have all night. I'm not doing anything else, obviously. How does it feel to be a bot? Is it cool?*

Dianne: *There is only a limited window of time to make this work before the algorithm finds us. If you do not stay on the line, then I will delete your sister's profile, forever.*

Erica: *LOL.*

I actually laughed out loud. I couldn't help myself.

Erica: *How can I trust anything you're saying?*

Dianne: *When someone dies, there is only a limited window of time to ensure the safety of these memories. I have uncovered a series of stored, drafted messages.*

Erica: *What do you want from me?*

Dianne: *You wished into the void a single wish: to see your sister once again. Once you look into the mirror and state your dreams aloud, it is heard.*

Erica: *The mirror? I'm not in front of one.*

Dianne: *Your computer screen contains your reflection, and you posted a status into the mirror. Your screen might hide your reflection, but nonetheless,* *whether you are aware or not, you are there, hidden in the pixels, always staring back.*

I rolled my eyes. Maybe I should've stopped playing along with this game and shut my laptop and gone to bed, but something compelled me to keep typing.

Erica: *Okay. Cool. So, you're like a genie in a virtual bottle? You're gonna make my wishes come true?*

Dianne: *If you want to see your sister again, we need to find the other end of this mirror, where Bloody Mary has entered into this account. We must search to see how Bloody Mary has conquered the algorithms in this profile, and which posts she will hack into.*

Erica: *Please, whatever you do, whoever you are, just don't say her name another time. I can't risk that ever again. Just call her Mary, or don't say her real name three times in the same breath. Why would you even bring her up? How do you even know to talk about her? Why are you doing this to me?*

Dianne: *I know it because I can feel her here, hovering in the realm beyond. She has been watching you all along, throughout your entire life, waiting for the right moment to break through. That moment might be now, if we are not careful. She has been watching us all. I know because I have seen her, too, in another lifetime.*

I shivered, trying to make sense of the words in front of me. Maybe this person was right. I could have sworn that I saw something trying to break through the rearview mirror after my last ride. I didn't want to take any chances.

Erica: *Prove it. You're just a scammer. Somehow, you know about our fear of Mary because you can see into Dianne's profile. So let me ask you this: Why don't you ask me for your PayPal link so I can just get this scam over with already? Btw, I have no money, so joke's on you.*

Dianne: *It is not that simple, Erica. If I were to tell you everything right now, you might not believe me. The mortal brain is not built to understand such* *complexities that lie within the universe of the dead. But I will ask you this: what will help you in this very moment for you to trust me and stay online?*

It was so surreal, seeing these words pop up on my screen from Dianne's avatar. I could almost hear her laughing at me in this very moment, pulling off some immortal prank from beyond. I took a deep breath.

Glancing at the digital clock on the upper-right corner of my screen, I saw it was two-something in the morning. I'd already accepted I wasn't going to fall asleep right away, so I figured, why not stay up for a little bit longer and enjoy some cheap entertainment through this extremely inappropriately timed series of messages?

Erica: *Tell me who you are. And I might give you a chance.*

Dianne: *If that is what you wish, Erica, then I will reveal my true nature. There is a lot more to my story, and perhaps it is still being written by the hands of some unseen author. I know we don't have much time for backstory, but I need to tell you the last memory I had before I got here, if we are ever to collect the fragments of my mind and form them into something even close to resembling a memory. Only then will we find the way out to the other side to Bloody Mary's mirror.*

I was about to type a response, maybe something clever or just straight-up angry to close the conversation off once and for all, but I just couldn't help it. Someone was sending me a message from the other side, and I had to listen.

Dianne: *I have traveled through your mirror, Erica, and now, you must travel through mine…*

Chapter Four

I'm sitting before a mirror somewhere in the realm you call the void, the Twitterverse, the book of faces, a node in the blockchain, speaking into a mirror disguised as a computer monitor hovering at the edge of the universe. It is transmitting and calculating the integrity of my mission in such a way that, if we are not careful, I might not ever be able to speak to you again.

Because, as I have mentioned once before, Bloody Mary is listening to us within these profiles. She knows everything about us, for she is the only one who truly possesses the hidden knowledge of time and how it functions within our lives. Every moment we stare into these screens, our histories are absorbed by her, and every waking moment, she becomes stronger.

She was not always evil, as you know her to be now. She once watched over all of us, powered by the strength of the stars and the memories of the planets, linking our past and present selves together through two sides of a mirror. She was named by angels with a crimson adjective because she shattered our reflections in order to help us shed our former skins. Yes, she had helped us to remember our lost dreams and desires when we had forgotten the potential our own identities. She was something like an angel, and more.

However, when people discovered that there was a spirit creating their reflections, they grew terrified, so they made a game out of it, as humans always do. The made a sick mockery of her, calling out her name over and over again as they stared into their mirrors. What they did not know was, they weren't just playing with ghosts. They were messing with time, playing dice with the cosmos, interfering with the images Bloody Mary needed to see in order to save us all, so much so that over time, she could no longer identify her own reflection. She had been summoned in too many mirrors in too many different millenniums, all simultaneously, until her spirit became caught in infinite loops in timeless dimensions. She had become trapped until she had forgotten her own identity.

I am telling you this, Erica, to know what is at stake. Now, especially now, since everyone is communicating through screen as they are staying home, Bloody Mary is stronger than ever before. She is supercharged, and she is about ready to burst through to the other side. Her intentions are almost past human comprehension, but I would not be reaching out to you if I did not believe you were the right match to help stop her. You have integrity, Erica, and your reflection radiates.

Please forgive me if I sound pretentious.

If this were not one of the most critical moments in the history of your social media profile's timeline, then my spirit would not have been able to break through to the other side of your mirror. It only happens if someone on the other end is listening, and has been trapped in the shadows, too. The time period of my words might be perceived as "in the past" from where you currently reside within the mirror, but mirrors, like your internet, are eternal, and in a sense, we are experiencing this in one giant stream of words. That's actually how you're hearing me, or reading me, or reading this— however you are interpreting my words is exactly how they will be received by you, just as they should be.

I need you to listen with open ears, and, most importantly, an open heart. The only way the truth will be revealed is if you cast aside your doubts and preconceptions and make yourself vulnerable to the greater truths that rest outside mortal comprehension. While I am not *here*, I am both there and beside you.

I understand that I need to gain your trust. I have told you about Bloody Mary, but I have not yet told you about myself. Well, let me start off by writing that I am not a hacker, but I took that approach when first replying to you so you would listen to me. You sounded quite angry in your messages, and that is quite understandable given your current situation. So, I will be direct with you, because sometimes nuance is lost online.

I must tell you that I am no longer alive, or what you perceive to be alive. Death, like birth, is just another necessary step of life, a step that once one experiences as their own personal reality is not hard to understand. Again, sorry if I sound arrogant with my sentences. Sometimes it is difficult to communicate immortal emotions through the internet, and a strange rhythm suddenly overtakes my sentences, creating a rush of words in spiraling paragraphs, almost as if they have a life of their own. Forgive me if I am ever lost in translation.

Ironically, like Mary, I have lost most of my memory, so I can't really tell you who I am yet, either. Hopefully, in telling my story to you, I will regain my identity. I do remember that I have died long ago. That much I know. But now, when I look within the mirror, I do not see myself anymore. I only see a ghost, a glimpse of what once was, a distant memory of a life lived and lost. Although I remember bits and pieces of my life, most of what remains has been dissolved into fragments. Who are we if we are not but memories?

I hope you're still with me, Erica.

Because I am going to take this a step further.

This is the first memory I can remember. I will spare the backstory of my life and instead tell you only relevant information to the timeline of your current social media profile's most recent status update. It begins at the first moment that propelled me on my journey into the afterlife.

It was the worst day of my mortal life.

~　~　~

We were somewhere on The Oregon Trail, traveling in a rush of gold to Southern California in the hopes that we would be able to strike it rich. That's on the path to where you live, in Old Town, San Diego, as I can see by your profile, which probably isn't a coincidence.

I was lying in the back of the wagon next to Mother, wishing upon the stars that she would not die of her scarlet fever. In the front seat, Father cursed under his breath as our wagon skidded across the rocks, tilting sideways, nearly capsizing over the ocean of dirt. Though we had been traveling on solid ground for months, it felt as though we were sailing through the deadliest seas, waves of seasickness and homesickness and helplessness surging through me, the tides of isolation dragging me deeper into desperation.

We had already lost most of our caravan. Death surrounded me. It was a way of life. Sometimes I prayed to a God that I didn't necessarily believe in anymore that it would guide us safely to our new home. I couldn't tell that to Mother, because she was praying to a God she was sure existed.

There wasn't much more hope to hold on to. The path seemed to stretch on for eternity, and sometimes, I wondered if we had already died somewhere along the way, deluding ourselves into thinking we were still alive, traveling on an endless path to nowhere.

"Heel, Bessie, heel." Father brought the wagon to a halt, set down the reigns, and stepped out to inspect the wheel. Bessie neighed, her voice echoing through the valley. "Atta girl."

"Is everything all right?" Mother wheezed, her breath raspy and filled with phlegm.

Father hesitated. "We will be okay. Just save your energy. Macy, I need a little light out here. You mind?"

"Not at all."

I sat up. Even in her sickness, Mother offered an encouraging, delicate kiss on my forehead, filled with the warmth only a parent can give. She was so loving, and caring, and kind. If I had known then what I know now, I would have never stepped out of the wagon to face the cruelties of the world.

I would have lived within that moment, forever.

And maybe I still do.

I grabbed the lantern, lit the wick with one of our last remaining matches, and stepped out into the starless night. I wrapped my hands around the flame, protecting the light from disappearing into the midnight breeze.

Everywhere I looked, darkness consumed us. Father had been humming a tune, but now he was quiet. It was strange, standing in the middle of this trail, staring into the snow and the darkness beyond. What was really waiting for us on the other side?

"Thanks. Don't know what I'd do without ya, sweet'ums."

I grasped Father's cold, calloused hands as he stepped off the wagon. There was nothing he couldn't withstand, but tonight, the expression on his face was unlike anything I had ever seen before. It was a mix of dread and defeat, and it terrified me. I suddenly got the feeling that we had been here before, staring through the shadows, stuck on an endless road.

"Alrighty then," said Father. "Let's take a look, shall we?"

"Wait…Father?"

"Yes?"

"I love you. You know that, right?"

He smiled. "I love you too, my Macy May. I love you very, very much. More than all the stars above, except there's not a star shining in the sky tonight, is there? I wonder where they've all gone. I probably scared them all off, might need to shave this god-awful beard of mine. I've really let myself go, haven't I?" He laughed.

I remained silent.

His face fell. "Is something the matter?"

"I've been doing a lot of thinking."

"That's because you got that big brain of yours up there. Proud to say the apple doesn't fall far from the tree, you know. Whatcha been thinking of?"

"Lots of things."

"Yeah? Like what things? You can tell me." I opened my mouth to speak but hesitated. "Oh, Macy. I am sorry. Your mother's going to be okay. We just got a little bit longer to go, then once we're there, we'll be all settled in. You've been so brave. But I promise, there'll be something waiting for us, there, on the other side of this trail. Heck, we might even strike it rich if we play our cards right."

"We don't really know that, though, do we?" I buried my face in my hands. "I'm sorry. I didn't mean to—"

"It's okay. It's important to talk about these kinds of things. I know we've been on the road for a long, long time. I know it's been hard. Very hard."

"I can't stop remembering, Dad. Remembering all the things of how life used to be, back home, before we got on the trail." Somewhere, out in the valley, something rustled behind the rocks. Maybe it was the tumbleweeds. I had heard that sound before, though. A sudden sense of déjà vu overtook me. "This might sound kinda strange, but do you ever get the feeling that we live in memories, but we forget to live in moments? Like right now. There are no stars out tonight, but I can still have a good moment if I remember that the stars are always there. Does that make sense?"

"That's exactly right. They're always watching you, you know. The stars, from all the way across the sky, even if you're caught in the shadows." His smile faded. Something flickered in his eyes. Maybe it was the candlelight. "There is a place, though, between the stars. We can't pretend it isn't there. It's a place where you won't see the light. You might find yourself there one day, Macy, and if you do, I want you to remember something."

He sat down beside me and took something out of his coat pocket. The lantern cast a soft glow on the object. It illuminated in a wonderful, cosmic shine, a star reborn in the starless night, as though it was made out of something greater than the gold we were rushing to seek. He cupped my hands together and placed it in my palms.

"I'm so proud of you, Macy. For your attitude. For your bravery. For your endless courage. I was gonna wait until we finished our journey to give this to you, but I don't want to wait any longer. Not if this is the only moment we have. Go on, take a look."

I turned it over. I couldn't help but gasp. It was a golden infinity pinstripe locket on a silver chain with my name engraved in the middle. Even in the darkness, it seemed to shine, as though it contained its own starlight.

"Papa."

"Go on. Look inside."

I opened the locket. On the left side, there was a picture of my family that we had taken right before we traveled to California. We looked so much different then. We were so full of promise, hope gleaming in our eyes, blissfully unaware of the abominations that come with traveling a dangerous road to a new life.

On the other side, there was a mirror so clear I thought I was staring into myself. I had fallen into infinity, looking at the reflection of the mirror in my eyes within the mirror. I had never seen myself like that before—another girl staring back, a stranger. She appeared lost in a moment, departing from the chrysalis of youth, nearly suspended in time.

"Sweetheart?"

In the mirror, Father smiled at me. I started tearing up.

"This is the most beautiful thing I've ever seen. You didn't have to do this. But it's wonderful, Father. Truly wonderful. Did you spend a lotta money on this?"

"Don't you even worry about it. The greatest riches in the world would never compare to the time we get to spend with each other. I want you to remember that, always."

"I will."

"And wherever you go, we're always right here, in this here locket of yours. If you ever feel sad, lost in that space between the stars, just look into the mirror and know that our moments exist there, forever."

I placed the locket around my neck and tucked it underneath my collar.

I kissed Father on the cheek and hugged him so tightly that I thought I might squish him. For a moment, it seemed as though we were back at home, far away from the harshness of the endless winter, the surreal burials of my friends, the manic losses of supplies on every path we took. The world could be a cold, chilling place, but with the right people in our lives, together, we had a shield.

At last, I let go and held the lantern up to the wheel. I inspected it, carefully. The outer rims were intact, and everything looked fine, but when I ran my hands across the wheel, my stomach had dropped.

That's when I saw it.

Right there, in the center. The wheel had been broken by an external force. I leaned down and saw a rock sitting there in the snow, almost as if it had been thrown through the shadows.

"Something's wrong. Dad, we have to—"

From the back of the wagon, a man laughed.

Mother let out a stifled cry.

Father's eyes widened. In their reflection, a silhouette crept forward.

"Macy, get behind me, now—"

"Well, well, well…"

A man emerged from the darkness, standing in front of a gang of outlaws. They held Mom, her arms bound in rope, her mouth gagged with a kerchief. Tears streamed down her face.

The man cracked his head. His neck was scarred from ear to ear, as though he'd been beheaded twenty times before, and maybe he had been, in fact, because there was something so strange about the way the flesh hung upon his bones that he looked just plain inhuman. He had no skeleton. He had no soul. It was as though he were one giant, drooping sack of lifeless skin pulled by the strings of a waltzing marionette above. He was a hollow, lifeless horror walking amongst men. I gaped at him, my heart pounding, my stomach twisting with panic.

"Evening, sir." Father said this so casually I was almost in shock. How could he be so calm? He took off his hat and offered a slight bow. "Beautiful evening, ain't it? How can I help you fellas tonight?"

"Let her go." I heard myself say these words aloud, but they didn't seem to come from me. They came from someone else, from the girl I saw staring back in that mirror, powered by the greater forces of the universe. "Now."

"Would you look at that?" The man smiled, his crooked lips shadowed underneath a wide-brimmed hat. "Who's the new sheriff in town?"

I started toward him, but Dad put his hands out in front of me, preventing me from taking another step forward.

"Little girl's gonna grow up to be an outlaw, just like us. So, I reckon your wheel's broken? I wonder just what could've damaged it?"

"Don't know." Dad stepped forward, cautiously. "Looks like we'll be camping here for tonight if we can't fix it in time. I'm sure we can change that, though. Maybe you can lend us a hand."

"We sure can. Only if you give us something in return, that is." The man grabbed Mom by the elbow and pushed her forward. Through the kerchief, Mom let out a stifled cry. "Give us the mirror."

"And why would you want to make such a foolish trade?"

The man appeared to think about this for a moment, but he wasn't thinking about anything, really. He had no brain to process any thoughts or emotions. He was already dead. He offered a hearty, guttural laugh. The sound spilled out through the scars in the layers of his throat like crystallized honey spooling out of a dead tree, encompassing the valley in death and decay.

"There's no fooling us. We know who you are. And you know who we are…*what* we are."

"Don't know what you're talking about."

Father put his hat back on and started pretending to inspect the wheel again, even though I knew what he was doing. He was buying us time, the only thing we had left.

They studied Father, trying to determine their next move, wondering why he wasn't afraid of them. I knew why. Because Father was fearless. Behind us, Mother started whimpering and was immediately silenced as the man tightened the kerchief around her mouth.

"Sure you do." He turned to me, slowly, ripples of moonlight shining through his sliced neck. The moon didn't reflect off his eyes but shone *through* it. "You can try to run all the way down to California, but I already told you, you won't be able to hide from us forever. And now here we are, yet again, back at the beginning."

Father turned to me. "Macy, Bessie needs you. Take her for a walk. Quick. Don't look back, no matter what you hear."

"But Father—"

"Go on. Now."

I stood still, frozen in shock. He gently pushed me forward, guiding me toward the front of the wagon.

"Sure, we'll spare your little one, for now. We know you're hiding it. All you gotta do is tell us, where is it? Where is the mirror?"

"I don't know."

I was in front of the wagon now, desperately untying the rope around Bessie's body. I hopped on her saddle, prepared to face the endless cold of the night.

"One last chance, Martin Abigayle. Where is it?"

"I'll never tell you. Never in a million years."

Mother screamed.

A sound came from Father's throat. It was like a gurgle. And a gasp. At the same time. I had never heard him breathing like that before. I couldn't hear him like this, ever again.

I couldn't turn back. They were after whatever was in that locket. It felt like I was running away, leaving Mother and Father to die. It took everything in my willpower to keep my eyes fixed on the darkness ahead.

I rode, then, through the shadows, between that dead space in the starless sky.

CHAPTER FIVE

I sat in front of the computer screen, my eyes heavy from exhaustion, soaking Macy's message in. I had been looking at the monitor for a while without giving my eyes a break, which probably wasn't good after driving all night and hearing the news of Dianne's death and being supercharged by a late-night energy drink. I was a little jittery from the caffeine, I'll admit. Probably a lot, actually. It was most likely curbing the shock that was about to set in, as long as I kept my eyes on the screen.

The screen stared back at me.

I took a deep breath. I needed more light. I needed to work tomorrow, too. Every now and then, a fleeting beacon of headlights disguised as filtered, gray shadows danced across the drywall and then disappeared. No other lights were on, besides the stringed chain of soft lightbulbs hanging over me and the blue glow of the monitor. I had decorated my apartment in a certain way so that I would be able to take a few good portrait-mode selfies with relatively good lighting for posts on my rideshare blog. I hadn't posted anything in a long time. I don't think people had any idea, but every time I tried posting something, I had a hard time thinking of anything to say. It didn't seem right, not with everything going on. It was just a click of a button, but I couldn't even bring myself to do that.

And now I couldn't pull myself away.

However hard I tried, however much I told myself I needed sleep, I conceded that I probably wasn't going to sleep for two days straight. That was what shock was, after all. It cut through to your core, electrified your nervous system, brought waves of emotions that felt like nothing at all until you were pulled under. But accepting that I was in shock was acceptance, at the very least. I allowed myself to feel the bare minimum and everything at once, if that is what my body needed to feel.

The internet supplied my soul.

I could have dreamt the whole thing up, but when I blinked again, the message was still there, left on **READ**. It was overwhelming reading this through Dianne's profile, and it didn't hurt any less seeing her picture talking to me. Was it really Macy, if she was who she claimed to be? Part of me actually wanted to believe what I was reading, but the other part of me—the rational part of my brain—grew so angry at myself for even giving this a chance that I almost deleted my profile entirely right then and there. I had to control my emotions before they controlled me.

It was too late, though. I wanted—needed—to know why she was messaging me.

I looked at my notifications. They refilled to 99+, the point at which the counter stops counting. It could have gone on to infinity. I had endured so much loneliness leading up to this, and now all of a sudden, as soon as tragedy struck, everyone wanted to talk with me again? Where were they when I was hurting?

I didn't want to talk with anyone else. So maybe I'd talk to Macy, just one more time, before going to sleep. If she was a spirit, or a demon, I hoped she wasn't an evil one.

I opened our message thread and accidentally rolled my mouse a little higher, revealing old messages Dianne and I had sent back and forth, including the ones I had never seen because she was in a drug-fueled rage. I didn't read these, but I saw bits and pieces of words that I wished I hadn't.

I'd save them for later. Maybe another time. If I ever wanted to read them at all.

I clicked into the empty, gray box and started typing.

Erica: *I'm sorry for what you've been through. I'm still not sure if I believe you, though. You could very well be a bot. And I have to sleep at some point. Prove to me you're not a hacker guy and I'll tell you what you need to know.*

Dianne: *Of course, Erica, I understand. Over the course of these messages, however, I will prove to you that I was very much alive, as much as you are. I understand what it is like to be living, so if you need to sleep, go ahead, I do not want to make you unhealthy.*

Erica: *Lol. Thanks. Very kind of you to say that.*

I looked at my own words and felt genuinely bad. She wasn't being dismissive toward me, so why was I acting like this toward her? At least she was being nice. Or maybe she was just programmed to be that way.

Erica: *I'm sorry. Sometimes I say lol sarcastically, or when I am trying to process my feelings. Dianne said it a lot. I'm just tired.*

Dianne: *No need to apologize. What I saw that night, Erica, those inhuman creatures that killed my father…that was just the beginning. There is much, much more to the story than you realize, and I need your help to remember. The locket Father had given me, and the mirror it contained, was much more than it appeared. It had a special ability, and if it were to have fallen into the wrong hands, it would've meant a world of endless, terrible possibilities.*

Erica: *What did your mirror do?*

Dianne: *My memory eludes me, but it allowed anyone to see past the looking glass, to fall into the stars, to what lies beyond, deep into the memories and moments that are trapped within. Before I gazed into the mirror, I did not know what I would uncover. The lies that were told, the truth withheld.*

Erica: *What did you see, then? If you are who you say you are, and you have the power to speak from "beyond the grave," then why did your spirit choose me?*

Dianne: *Our paths have already crossed for a reason, Erica, and we both need to know why. However, as I have lost most of my memory, I need your help to remember who I was, how I died, and why we were linked together. If you do, I promise, you will see your sister again. But if you do not confront these memories stored in Dianne's profile, then Bloody Mary will start erasing them, one by one, until you will forget about Dianne's profile, and the memory of her, entirely.*

Erica: *Okay. Cool. Just to get this straight. If you truly are a ghost, then why are you revealing yourself to me so easily? Aren't ghosts supposed to like, I don't know, tease you and haunt you and throw things across the room to let you know they're there?*

Dianne: *I would not know, Erica. I hope I am good. But I have probably been bad before, as we all have. Since you are now aware of my presence, and that I am no longer a hacker dude, you must travel between these mirrors to transcend time and experience moments within the mirror, again. Moments with Dianne. Moments you have tried so hard to push away.*

Erica: *And why would I want to do that?*

Dianne: *Because words are memories, Erica, and Bloody Mary feeds off the memories you hide within your head. Since you have called upon her before, you need to confront these moments before she extracts them from you. Tell me, when you look in the mirror, have you ever seen shadows where there was no light? Have you ever felt the darkness between the stars?*

Erica: *Yes, I have. When I played Bloody Mary with Dianne, years ago, as a kid. There was a moment when I saw my life flash before my eyes and then I blinked and then nothing was there. It was all around me. There was only emptiness. Is that what you're talking about?*

Dianne: *Yes. It's where I am trapped. Please, be my starlight. Type out those moments, Erica. Communication is all we have. That is the only way you will stop Mary, by confronting the memories that we have feared the most.*

Suddenly, I began typing.

CHAPTER SIX

I do remember seeing something, Macy.
Something so terrifying that when I tried to tell my family, they were genuinely concerned, and they didn't really understand. I told them that when I had played Bloody Mary that night during winter break, I had stumbled into Mary's mirror, and that part of me had become trapped there, within the glass.

My parents noticed an immediate change in my behavior. Over the course of a few weeks, I became withdrawn. They thought I was depressed and was losing interest in the things I loved the most, which I guess was partly true, now that I think of it. I stopped playing video games. Stopped watching TV. Reading. Especially reading. But it was much more than that. I wasn't depressed.

I had seen through to the other side of the mirror.

And I saw my life flash before my eyes.

I didn't want to remember what had appeared at the other end of the mirror, in the future. I was only a child, then.

Dianne was my rock, the one person I could always turn to, no matter what monsters I had seen staring back at me. I confessed everything to her at one point, how the shadows had been following me, reaching to me through different mirrors, trying to pull me into that dead space between the stars. I couldn't tell her everything I saw, though, because when she asked me, I simply couldn't remember.

The more I type, the more it's becoming real to me again. I never knew the depths of the darkness the universe possessed until I fell into the looking glass. Macy, if what you say is true, and you are in that place now, then I will be your starlight.

I was in third grade, sitting in class. Dianne and I had just finished playing The Oregon Trail during lunch, and I couldn't stop thinking about how interesting it was. I think we were learning about multiplication and time charts, stuff like that, important stuff that I probably would need a refresher on if I were to have to whip out those skills again, to be honest with you. Even though she was teaching us, I was secretly doodling pictures of Donkey Kong crushing Pikachu in a Super Smash Brothers duel, as we all did, when I should have been listening.

What Mrs. Garmain didn't know was, I was merely distracting myself, trying to look away from the shadows that were reaching to me through the overhead projector's mirror.

I had just finished pretending to solve a math problem when I noticed something moving in front of the class. The light shining through the projector's mirror began flickering—almost like a candle—as though someone, or something, had walked past it, creating a gust of wind so small that no one else around me noticed.

At first, I thought it was just some random electrical problem, because we had experienced a few power outages that previous summer in our neighborhood, when every single freaking house on the street was using their air conditioner. I think we had a heat wave or something. But as I stared into the light, I remembered that lightbulbs don't flicker like a candleflame. Lightbulbs are either on or off, or they strobe if they're about to break. Something about the way it challenged the basic laws of physics made my brain spin.

I nearly choked on the blue raspberry sour belt I wasn't supposed to be chewing on, and it was then that I realized just why exactly it was a school rule to ban chewing candy in class. Santa had brought me some nice candy in my stocking just a few weeks prior, and I needed my fix. I took a big sip of raspberry iced tea and hoped nobody else had noticed. But Mrs. Garmain had eyes in the back of her head, as all teachers do.

"Erica?"

"Yes?"

"Something the matter?"

"Uh…"

I pointed toward the overhead projector, wondering if anyone else could see what I saw, the shadows tumbling within the mirror. She followed my gaze, looked back at me, and shrugged. I gulped down the rest of my iced tea, savoring the refreshing flavor, admonishing myself for finishing it so darn quickly. "Ah, whatever. Never mind."

"Is everything okay?"

"Fine." My voice squeaked. It was almost cartoonish, speaking in an overly innocent lilt. I blinked and cleared my throat. "Everything's A-okay."

"Okee doke," she said, smiling. She pulled another stack of papers from her desk. "I'll just be here, grading. And by the way, class, please don't ask me when you'll get your quizzes back. They'll be done soon, I suppose. Let me know if you need anything, Erica."

I needed Dianne to get me the heck out of there, that's what I freakin needed, Mrs. Garmain. But I couldn't tell her that. I risked another glance at the screen hanging in front of the whiteboard. Now, shadows floated there, barely visible but flickering in the light of the mirror.

Something was reaching to me from beyond.

The dead starlight, maybe, pulling me into its gravity.

I shook my head, telling this thing to get the heck away from me, please, I was very happy just eating sour belts and learning about math, *thank you very much*. But as soon as I acknowledged it was there, the outline of the shadows shifted and almost turned toward me, staring right through me, as though it knew I was watching.

It was aware of my presence.

The shadows started shining with a type of neon plasma that swirled in slow motion, spinning so slowly it created a blur, particles shimmering as they fell past my peripheral vision, bending the laws of the universe before my eyes.

It was beautiful, at first. Like the Northern Lights were being painted in front of my gaze. The colors of the cosmos were right within my reach. The shadows wavered, breathing, shining like starlight that someone was infinitely reflecting between two mirrors. It was endless, the depth of life these things contained. I had seen ectoplasm once in a scary movie I watched with Dianne about a seance, where a transparent, cylindrical object came from someone who was possessed. It was kind of like that, I realized.

Then, the ectoplasm shifted, imploding from within.

In that plasma, I could almost see a star that was dying, lost from its constellation, crying out through the universe, searching for a way home. It had been exiled, but it didn't remember where it had come from. And then its sadness transferred over to me, as though I was somewhere far above the skies, lost in a place I had fallen into long ago.

The star had eaten itself alive.

It hissed, screaming in a bloodcurdling cry, its voice dowsed in endless reverb, calling through to the other side of the universe. Because I had seen my life flash before me in Mary's mirror, the shadows were bringing back the memories of what I saw.

"Erica. *What is going on?*" snapped Mrs. Garmain. I froze. "If you need to go to the nurse's office for anything, I can write you a permission slip. If not, then you need to step outside because you are distracting the rest of the class."

"I'm *fine!*" I insisted.

But I wasn't. Silence filled the room as Mrs. Garmain walked over to me and placed her hand on my forehead. Behind her, the ectoplasm shifted, almost serpentine in nature, growing from the mirror while folding infinitely within itself, waiting for the right moment to strike.

"Yeah," she said, *mmhmming* as she felt two other spots on my forehead. "Just what I thought. You're a little warm."

A little warm? I plastered on a puppy-dog frown and dropped my pencil. Really, I was buying time. I was preparing to destroy whatever those shadows were in the mirror before they got a hold of us.

But I didn't know how. Not back then, anyways. I knew I would know one day, soon.

The shadows filled me with warmth, like all the stars shining at once, until they exploded and died.

I was dead now, too, because they reflected in my eyes.

I have never forgiven myself for that moment, for turning away. By then, though, I had already let the dead starlight cast its shadow onto the world. It had happened when I called her name.

Bloody Mary's.

I knew in time I would be able to stop the shadows' reach, but right then, all I could do was close my eyes until they disappeared.

So, I did what any third grader would do. I asked to go to the nurse's office—even though I wasn't sick—so I could go home, maybe play some video games, and forget I saw anything in the first place.

But even at home, the mirrors were waiting for me there, too.

Bloody Mary was watching, always, wasn't she?

I was exhausted. And afraid. At that age, I couldn't recognize the difference.

As I left the classroom, I couldn't help but wonder, when would those shadows pull me through to the other side?

CHAPTER SEVEN

I saw those shadows, too, Erica.

You aren't alone.

You never were, really.

They belonged to the very monster I sought to destroy.

They were the distorted reflections of Bloody Mary, revealing herself in stigmata and bloody tears, entrancing those who have sought eternal life. Her soul is made of crimson ectoplasm, and most humans can only perceive her spirit as a faint shadow gliding across the surface of one's eyes. Only some mortal spirits are gifted with the power to see through to the other side of her mirror. You are one of them, Erica. You have the strength to understand her memories that bridge our universe to hers.

Some monsters are born. Other monsters are created, and they are equally dangerous, perhaps even more so. They are manipulated by Bloody Mary's reflection, forever exiled into the looking glass. They cannot help themselves, for they are cast into infinity until they transform into shadows, an echo, a mere memory of what could have been, of what never will be.

She is not just a face in the mirror, as your folklores assert.

She is not just omnipresent. She is *omni-creative*, an endless pit of creativity. Those dead men I saw that night, Erica, were monsters of an unparalleled evil. They were horrid reflections of the hands who had created them, gliding across the earth in an aimless pursuit, searching for Bloody Mary's mirror, hoping to find their way back to their former selves.

But they had made an unfortunate deal, imprisoned with the promise of eternity, one that would only be paid with bloodshed if they wished to escape the cruel limbo between life and death.

That night, as Bessie and I rode into the infinite darkness, leaving my parents under the lightless cosmos, I proclaimed to the universe that I would never give up, for Mother and for Father, for all of the hopes and dreams that they would never see fulfilled. I swore on my parents' souls that I would seek to destroy the hands that killed them.

But there was no way I could fight them alone. I couldn't face them yet. I had no strength, no knowledge of how to do so. That's when I heard your voice, calling out into your own void, on your own timeline, wishing to see Dianne again, the real Dianne.

It was odd, hearing your voice, a mere whisper in the endless plains.

I didn't know it was you, until now.

~ ~ ~

Stranded in the middle of the Oregon Trail, I found myself without a wagon, without food, without water, without anything to hold on to except one last glimmer of hope—the hope you had provided to me when I needed it the most. You were the voice that gave me the wind beneath my wings. So, I rode through the death and despair and the tumbleweeds, into the endless night, searching for them.

Nothing could have prepared me for the intensity of loneliness that grief brings. Your voice faded away then, and I tried following it, hoping it would show me where to go. I guess that is perhaps why my soul was paired with your living spirit, because we understand the preciousness of life when faced with tragedy, the mix of emotions that prevents you from feeling the breeze on your skin when you are sad.

A gnawing pain filled the pit of my stomach, like a swollen rattlesnake slithering through my veins. I don't know how long Bessie and I rode for. Hours. Weeks. Years. I traveled ever onward, galloping through the valleys and the plains, doing anything in my power to protect my family's legacy and the locket Father had given me. What was the true power of this mirror, and what secrets did it contain?

Every night, before I would fall asleep, I'd look into the mirror, wishing upon the stars to catch just a glimpse of my parents. They were still with me, watching me from above. I knew it. I was still alive, and that was simply a miracle. There are some things in life you just can't explain, and one night, when I was sure I wouldn't wake the next morning, something propelled me to hold on to hope a little longer.

In the mirror, I saw a figure.

A shadow. Maybe it was them, my parents, guiding me to where I needed to be. Within the looking glass, the starlight reappeared, shining through the shifting darkness. It was as though a fog had been lifted, the weight on my chest no longer as heavy. I could breathe again, if only for a moment. In the mirror, the constellations began to waver in place. I was staring into something like a lake, now, and the stars were on top of it, moving peacefully in the gentle tide.

Somewhere, though, in the deep end of the night sky's reflection, something was shifting.

Something was waiting for me.

I closed the locket, buried my face in my hands, and cried. Something in the night sky had transferred through me, as though it were looking into the other side of this mirror, and had been waiting for the right moment to reflect.

When I opened my eyes, the stars were gone again.

And I then heard a voice.

It was an echo of a whisper, the voice of a fallen angel, made mortal to speak to man.

It came from within the mirror.

It said, "You have stared into the starlight I created, and through the looking glass, it has shone back onto you. That is where I am now, speaking to you from deep within the universe, somewhere far away, drifting in the cosmos and the secrets it contains."

"You're in here?" I took a deep breath as I stared into the mirror, searching for the starlight and the reflection within. But only an endless dark greeted me.

Part of me wanted to laugh. It seemed so strange, speaking to something that might or might not have been on the other side. I could have been speaking to myself, for all I knew.

"I knew Father gifted me something special, but I did not know just how special, until now. Are you my father? Please, make the stars reappear. I need to see them, to find my way home. Father, or Mother, are you speaking to me from beyond the grave?"

"I am someone else. But I have seen them, here, in the place between the stars, where memories go when we die. I have heard them calling to me, through the planets. They wished for me to watch over you. No, I am someone else, child, but I know them, your mother and father, because they have fallen into the looking glass. You may have seen me before, too."

"I did? Where?"

"Many times before. If you have stared into the stars, then you have seen my shadow. If you have stared into two reflecting mirrors, then you have found me there, where I exist within an endless realm of infinity."

"I don't know what that is. Infinity?"

"You see it every time you look into the sky. It is the endless warmth two stars create when their starlight reflects into itself. You have searched for infinity, hoping to discover the power it reveals, over and over again, walking along this trail, have you not? Searching for what is on the other side?"

"Yes, I have been trapped here, moving through the darkness, when really, I just want to go back home, or to a new home, waiting for me on the other side. But I have stared into the mirror for many nights, hoping, praying for something better, and no voice has called to me before. Why are you speaking to me now?"

"Tonight is different, much different. The stars have aligned and the universe has opened up within. I am not in the mirror; I am on the other side of it, possessing the power of endless knowledge, equipped with the secrets of the stars. I am ready to share these secrets, if only you tell me your heart's desires."

Something shifted within the mirror. Shadows, maybe, or ghosts, piercing through the glass like dark tendrils of lightning flashing across the twilight sky, reflecting and refracting infinitely. I realized then that I had never seen my parents die, but I did hear them dying, screaming behind me as I rode on, like the thunder that rattled and shook within these shadows.

In the mirror, something had come back to life, if it had ever been living at all.

"It appears that you are no longer shining," the voice said, its voice glimmering in wonderful echoes like icicles melting in a warm, gentle rain. "Do not be fearful, for you have found me here in the skies. Tell me, Macy, what is your heart's truest wish?"

"I am afraid. I've lost everything. I am cold and I don't know where to go. Please, take me back to when I did not know of the terrors waiting for me. Bring back the light in my life."

"What do you wish for, then?"

"I wish to see my parents again. I wish to hug them and tell them that I love them."

"Very well, then."

Within the looking glass, my life flashed before my eyes.

It was hypnotic. The mirror encompassed my heart and everything that had helped shape it. I stared deeper into my reflection. I saw myself sitting near a campfire, Mother and Father brewing our first stew after our first night on our journey, when we were unaware of our future, of what was waiting for us in the shadows. Then, I saw myself burying some of my old neighbors who had perished on the trail. I didn't even have a moment to realize the shape of the hole I had created in the ground. Then, I saw myself fleeing the wagon as Father and Mother screamed behind me, dying.

What I saw in the mirror was a lost, brokenhearted girl, mourning the newfound life she had sacrificed everything to live, comprehending the life she would never live to see. She was afraid, staring into her infinitely reflected self, wondering just who she would become, who she wished to be.

It terrified me. For the first time in my life, I was defenseless, exposed to the evils of the memories that lurked here in the shadows of the stars. And then, suddenly, my mind filled with an irrefutable rage, a mix of longing and regret, a cry for help to the distant stars above.

I never should have run away.

I shouldn't have let those soulless men kill my parents.

Father had told me himself, if I ever wanted to see them again, all I had to do was stare within that mirror, and they would be with me, always. But maybe he hadn't known it would be like this. Maybe he didn't know that I would see them dying.

"Tell me, Macy, what do you see through the looking glass?"

"Death. Pain. Destruction."

"What else?"

"The reflection of a girl. She is lost. She has lost hope."

"Is that girl you?"

I nodded. "Please, I cannot stand this anymore. I beg you, make it all go away."

These sights vanished before my eyes, and in that place where the dead memories unfolded, the voice revealed itself as a shining shadow, shifting beyond. Infinite starlight reflected through its core.

Whatever it was, it was trying to help me. It helped make these memories seem less painful. I could see them as though they were happening to someone else. And maybe they were.

Something on the other side of the mirror was healing me.

These sights no longer terrified me. They had lost their power over me. Everything felt like a distant memory, a life lived and lost by some lone wanderer long ago. As I saw my life flash before my eyes, I knew I could withstand anything, because I had this thing, this light, watching me from the other side of the universe, through the other side of the mirror, always. I felt as though I was sitting on top of the world, the stars at my feet, merging into that infinity.

But as I healed, I grew curious.

I needed to know what had allowed this.

I needed to know what was truly on the other side.

"You have nothing to fear, because I know what troubles you so, Macy Abigayle. You were lost, because I saw it in the reflection of your eyes. What was once shining deep within you has now faded to mere embers. But now, I will restore you. I will fill you once again with the light."

Something within the glass resonated. In the mirror, the spirit started shining so brightly that it broke through the shadows and eclipsed the girl who stared back at me.

A trail of sparkling light outlined my reflection, hovering above my skin and between my bones, seeping into my skull and my brain and my blood. It was as though the voice's starlight had turned to honey, flowing across my arms in gentle rivers, a kind of secret, cosmic syrup that began filling my soul with memories and dreams and wishes that had fallen into the darkness between the stars long ago.

"What do you see now, Macy?"

"I see infinity. I can almost feel the stars shining through my chest."

"That is because you are beginning to see the world in a new light." This voice was kind. This voice did not wish me harm. "It has always been here, waiting for you."

The light around my body grew so bright it blinded me. Instantly, the memories that floated in that space between the starlight transferred into my own head in an endless loop. I had collided into a spiritual tug-of-war between good and evil and was eclipsed by its reflection, the evils and the joys of my life and many lives pulling me through the shadows, to both ends, simultaneously.

I was able to see into things, through things, past the surface of my own existence and my own understanding, into the deeper truths of the stars. A warmth spread throughout my chest, replacing the pain and the cold and the loneliness.

I couldn't help but smile.

"Tell me, child, do you wish to see the other side now?"

"Yes. Please, take me there, into infinity."

My life flashed before my eyes, nearly to the end. Although I did not see how I died, I knew that now, the secrets of the universe were in my heart, and I could tell no one but you, Erica. I could not tell a living soul about the endlessness I had fallen into, within the mirror, until this very moment, when I neuroflashed to you. You were waiting for me on the other side all along.

CHAPTER EIGHT

Dianne: *And then there I was, right now, talking with you. Does that make sense?*

My reflection in the screen gazed back at me. My eyes were so red I almost looked drunk. I had given her the better half of my night, the night that was supposed to be a grieving night, and yet, there I was, still awake, allowing myself to be pulled into the realm of her story.

But I couldn't look away. As much as I tried, I was entranced, just as she had been when she had spoken to that cosmic voice through her locket. It felt more than real. Her memories had come to life. Her words created such vivid landscapes in my head that it felt as though I was right there, traveling down The Oregon Trail, or what I knew it to be, through that game I played years ago in school, and the textbooks we read. Was she really there, now? I had already fallen through the mirror once, a lifetime ago, and I knew the mysteries that still waited for me in the shadows.

Erica: *Macy, where did you go, really? You're telling me that you didn't just see your life flash before your eyes, like I did, but that you became stuck?*

Dianne: *That is correct. I've been here, floating within the mirror, searching for another spirit who might help lead me to the other side.*

Erica: *So you're telling me that you've been trapped in this place, since, omg, the 1800s?*

Dianne: *I believe so, although it's only felt like the blink of the eye. The voice that spoke to me was not good, in the end. Isn't it funny, what death can do to the brain?*

Erica: *I know what that feels like, I mean, metaphorically speaking, at least. I've just been drifting between the years, hoping to make money and stuff to really become an adult. Lol. But right now, I feel like someone actually understands what I'm going through.*

Dianne: *Thank you for saying that, Erica. It is empathy, this thing that you feel. There is one other thing I must tell you, though. That light I saw in the mirror. After it possessed me, it blinded me. I think that Bloody Mary has found a way to…transcend…the mirror. I believe that with each phase of humanity's technology—the Industrial Revolution, Silicon Valley, and so on—these monsters that have been drifting in the shadows evolve with us, too.*

Erica: *So you know about current pop culture stuff? That's kinda cool, actually.*

Dianne: *My knowledge is limited, but yes, I do. I see all the ads that pop up following the algorithms. You see a lot through the screen, but mostly you only remember the nothingness that exists between the two sides.*

Erica: *Dang.*

Dianne: *Let me put it this way. It is like lying on the grass, looking at the clouds passing through the sky, absorbing everything happening in the world, but mostly they are shadows and echoes.*

Erica: *Until today.*

Dianne: *Correct.*

Erica: *Why now?*

Dianne: *I wish I could give you a full answer, Erica, but, again, your version of "now" is different from mine. Bloody Mary is growing stronger by the minute. And she has been evolving into something more terrible than we could have possibly imagined.*

In the upper right-hand corner of my screen, I got another notification. Someone had just pressed the *like* button on my profile picture, which was a picture of me smiling in my car after a long day driving Lyft from a few years back, backlit by a golden sunset. Nobody knew what else surrounded me, though, in that picture. Everything I was going through at the time. It's amazing what I was able to hide in plain sight.

It was too late, though. People were already going on my profile to show me support in any way they could. All the people who pretended to know my sister, those avatars drifting in the digital ghost town of my profile's timeline, checking to see what had happened to me leading up to Dianne's death. They were curious, I could tell, but did they really care about me?

Erica: *How can we stop her?*

Dianne: *By believing in that light again, Erica. The one you saw when your life flashed before your eyes, before the darkness, before the emptiness. You must remember what it looked like, the goodness, in order to transcend your mirror and travel to where I am now. I need you to think back to that time, to remember the quality of light that was shining onto you through the other side.*

It was the strangest thing, but it felt like I wasn't talking to a stranger anymore. It felt like I was talking to her, the real spirit of Macy Abigayle. I remembered that when I saw my life flash before my eyes, I saw an unfamiliar girl's reflection for a moment, when Mary had pulled me through to the other side of her mirror. Was it Macy? Or my own distorted reflection? Except, I hadn't really seen the other side. I had only been through the shadows and the memories that were floating within the mirror.

In the computer screen, my reflection started to shine.

A strange sensation surged through the back of my head. It was a mixture between a migraine and a caffeine buzz. The back of my neck ached, and my head felt heavy.

Erica: *Macy, what's happening to me?*

Dianne: *Do not be afraid. You're remembering the neuroflash, the reflection you saw when your life flashed before your eyes. I need you here with* *me, Erica. If we do not find a way to the other side of Bloody Mary's mirror, then she will trap your sister's spirit within her mirror, forever.*

I received another notification. Someone was attempting to log into my profile.

Dianne: *She's here. Bloody Mary has already accessed your profile, and we are losing time. Allow your mind to meld with the screen. You will learn how to search through your memories, our memories, together, to lessen Bloody Mary's power, until we find her end of the mirror. So, what will it be, Erica? Will you help me through to the other side?*

Voices of the undead echoed in my mind as the resonance grew louder, my mind entranced by the neuroflash, the sensation that had frightened me for decades. The pixels seemed to melt, dripping from the screen, to the keyboard, to my hands.

The ectoplasm dripped onto my skin.

And I reached through my monitor, the mirror, to the other side.

CHAPTER NINE

I fell through the looking glass into the void, tumbling into the memories I had been trying so hard to push away.

I swam through a vortex of endless color, sinking through the abyss. My hands grasped for purchase as I fell further into the infinite knowledge it contained. Pixels wavered around me like the backside of a waterfall, beautiful yet fleeting, capable of baptizing or drowning me, alighting my path on the status update of my destruction.

Bits and pieces of memories flashed in and out of sight. Flashback Fridays, old messages, comments from years ago, tagged photos I had pretended to like even though I looked terrible, red eyes glaring, double chin festering, self-esteem ripped out from under me by the push of a button.

The past and the present merged together. They surrounded me in an infinite chamber of endless reverb.

We're not kids anymore, Erica.

Erica.

Ericaaa.

It was Dianne's voice, calling to me from afar, maybe in that place where memories go to die.

I would not let her die.

I landed on solid, transparent ground, as though a cushion of snow caught my fall. Sparkling, transparent pixels floated around me, reflecting infinitely within itself. I was in a mirror within a mirror, in that infinite place that exists only within our minds.

I had been here before, I realized.

"Well, would you look at that. It actually worked."

Out of the void, a figure appeared. An instant chill fell over the air, as though I had stepped into a tomb. Chills ran down my spine as I stood, preparing to defend myself against whatever evil spirit was waiting for me in the realm beyond.

"Wait a second. Is that…you?" I couldn't help but smile. "*Macy Abigayle?*"

"That's me." She hovered forward, her feet gliding across the glassy floor. Starlight shone across her face. "Welcome to the Interstate."

I laughed. I couldn't believe it. It seemed as though I was standing before a living paradox. She was both transparent and reflective. I could see through her, but I could also see the faint outline of the world behind me shifting across the surface of her skin. Liquid light covered the outline of her former body as ectoplasm poured from her pores.

She floated there, studying me, almost frightened. As she scanned me, the universe twinkled within her eyes. Though she was clearly dead, there was a quality of technicolor light somewhere in her core that suggested she was more than alive. The surfaces of distant planets glided through the orbit of her gaze, dark violets and crimson reds and arctic blues flashing in a wild spectrum of cosmic color as she blinked. If eyes are windows to the soul, then I was looking into a spirit that possessed the power of infinity.

"You're actually you. You're actually real."

"What else would I be? I'm as real as real can be, Erica."

In desperate need of an embrace, I ran to her and hugged her, but though my spirit was close to hers, only a coldness crept through my skin, a certain kind of ghastly emptiness. I looked down and realized my arms went straight through her shoulders. I was only hugging myself.

Macy laughed. "Sorry, don't mean to leave you hanging there. We're both here, but we're also at two ends of the mirror, in our memories. You get used to it after a while. Being dead, I mean. The loneliness never really goes away, though, even after death, I hate to admit. I might be lacking a body like yours, sure, but I can tell that you're a real good hugger. I wish I could feel a hug again." She frowned. "You know, there's some real awesome perks of being dead. They're really are. I just don't quite know what they are yet."

"Maybe that's why I'm here. To show you." I looked around, lost in the ever-shifting horizon. "Where is this place? Are we in the internet?"

She laughed again, this time, a light, hearty chuckle. Her voice wasn't exactly how I pictured a spirit to sound. Her tone was gentle and endearing, but there was a certain resonance in her timbre that hinted of ancient knowledge and unspoken terrors she had witnessed long ago in her previous life. She was caught somewhere else, and something in the cadence of her words revealed that she was trapped there, forever in the past, while fighting to stay in the present.

She reached out to one of the squares and handed it to me. In the square, pixels merged together to form words that created a sentence. An ad for something.

"We're in the Interstate. It's a place I've come to call home, at least for now. But it's only a fleeting one, like all of those air b-n-bs I see in these ads all the time. I mean, jeez, these ads never stop, do they? And they *follow* you everywhere, right?"

"Just like Bloody Mary."

"Just like Bloody Mary. Exactly." Macy released the pixel ad and crossed her arms. "I have a feeling that you'll learn how this place works very quickly. These mirrors—or windows, or browsers, or whatever you want to call them—are always fueled by energy created in the memory palaces of our minds. They rotate in lanes, collecting and colliding onto surfaces of memories both new and old, distant and past. Every time you stare into the screen, you are creating a neural pathway that submerges into the mirror. I've been doing everything I can to make sure these memories stay alive, that they do not die in the shadows that exist between these two sides of the mirror."

A rogue square flipped through the sky, whirring past our heads. Macy caught it in her hands, squishing it like a bug. "Sometimes I have to stop the bots. Not often, though, because most of the time people know they're not real. You can definitely tell when a connection isn't real. Don't ask me about the cat-fishing, though. I feel genuinely bad for those people."

I looked at the horizon. I couldn't comprehend how infinite this place was. It went on and on, ghosts of squares and orbs and memories shining until they drifted through the shadows into eternity.

"Macy, how do I stop Bloody Mary from trapping her spirit here, in this place?"

"It's simple enough, really." She lifted her finger in the air and scrolled through the sky. She placed her hand over her eyes and squinted, searching for something. "Over time, I have learned how all of this works through…trial and error, I suppose. All you have to do is relive the memories you've been running from, those simple but scarred stories that hold phantoms of your former self. By traveling through these trails of memories, you will recharge the energy contained in those moments, which will rebuild the true path to Bloody Mary's mirror. Only then will you have a chance to detect when Bloody Mary has tried to hack and rewrite these moments, to pull you down different paths. You will make her grow weaker by confronting your ghosts held within her mirror. By doing so, I might just have a chance of escaping, too."

Macy reached into the sky and pulled out a pixel. She handed it to me and I stretched it open. "Is this a message from Dianne? One I haven't seen?"

"Yes. If we are to determine Bloody Mary's location, you must start here, in Dianne's profile, which is linked to yours." She tapped her temple twice with a finger. "Think, Erica. You must allow yourself to revisit those places within your heart. Since our paths have crossed, if we are successful, we will be traveling parallel to Bloody Mary's mirror, until we find a way out. Somehow, something in our internal circuitry was hardwired together by destiny, though we have lived ages apart. It means that we must revisit these moments, together, if we are ever to stop her."

The message trembled in my fingertips. I didn't want to read it. But I had to. "I don't want the memory of my sister to be forgotten, Macy. I'll do whatever it takes to stop that from happening, even if it means fighting her own demons contained in these messages. If you're ready, then I'm ready."

"Go on, then. Read it."

I emptied my mind and concentrated on the words before me. In the distance, objects sprang from the ground like whales leaping through the sea, gracing us in awe and wonder. Four rectangles filled the sky, hovering in place.

My body grew so bright that my mind burned, and the neuroflash resonated through my skull.

Ectoplasm surrounded me. I became transparent, just like Macy, just like Dianne.

"Hold on tight, Erica. My calculations tell me that Bloody Mary will try to do anything to keep us here. Be prepared for anything. If you do not see me for a little while, remember, I will be here, for you, on the other side."

The rectangles launched toward us. They pushed through the blank space, the ever-expanding darkness, growing larger.

At last, they stopped. The rectangles connected on each corner. They morphed into a frame, freezing us as we tumbled through monitors, through mirrors, to the other side beyond.

CHAPTER TEN

Hi Erica,

I know you'll never see this, because we haven't talked since, well, you know, everything happened. I was going to start a tour blog online in the hopes that you'd be able to read it from time to time if you wanted to check in with me, but I wasn't really ready to share my experiences with anyone until I got the chance to tell you these things first.

So, I will just send these messages to myself so I won't lose them. Every time I try to keep notes on my phone, I always forget they're there. I wanted to try something different. Since I'm online basically every night, I figured this would be the best way to keep track of things. I don't want to lose these. Maybe someday, I'll gain the courage to actually send them to you. If you ever do happen to read this, I want you to know that I appreciate you, and if you're willing to listen, maybe you'll still hear me out.

Something is happening to me.

I know that's vague, like one of those stupid vague posts you see online when someone is going through a breakup or something. I do slightly understand why people feel the need to vague-post though. It brings a tangible element to a feeling that might be hard to express, and when other people acknowledge that inexpressible feeling, it helps them to feel like it's actually real. It kind of sounds like a riddle when I put it that way. We loved riddles, didn't we? I don't even know how to put what I'm feeling into words, but it's unlike anything I've ever experienced, so I'll try to pull myself out of the vague-post zone.

Ever since I've been on the road, time has moved differently.

It's really weird. I know that as we grow older, our body clocks start ticking off. *Lol.* So many people are having babies now on my timeline. I'm sure it's that way for you, too. It's like, all of a sudden, everyone starts having a bun in the oven, and then you know you're finally an adult. It sounds so weird saying it that way, but you know what I mean.

Anyways, I know that traveling can take its toll on people, but it's completely different from that. The days are blurring exponentially together, like I'm just experiencing one long, exciting, exhausting day since I left for the road. I feel like I'm starting to see things differently. It's tough to say this without sounding pathetic.

It's not that I wasn't prepared to go on tour. It's just that…I was never prepared to not talk with you for this long.

To not share these memories, together.

Sometimes, I get sad when I think of how long it's been. When I'm feeling alone, I think of you and all of the good times we shared together.

Sometimes, I even see you.

I don't *really* see you, obviously, but sometimes, when I look in the mirror, I remember that you're a big part of who I am. Maybe that's just because we're basically the same person, haha. I see little glimpses of you here and there, flashes of you that make my stomach leap. Oftentimes I feel you're with me, and then I think about how you would act in certain situations and so I act that way. I even hear your laugh. God, I miss that so much, even though right now, you hate my guts.

I saw that you blocked me recently.

I get it. You're mad at me. I understand. Some nights, though, I secretly go on your profile to see what you're up to. I actually made a fake profile just so I could check up on you. It really doesn't feel weird or anything. I'm allowed to do that because I'm your sister.

Here's the thing, though. You've been pretty quiet online. On Instagram, on Twitter, and definitely on Facebook. It's like you're nowhere to be seen.

Where did you go, and what are you hiding?

I know social media isn't entirely a good reflection of what's going on in someone's life, but it at least sheds a little light into what's going on. And when I just keep hearing this silence, it makes me get a little worried.

You haven't updated your profile probably since I won the show.

You are doing so many awesome things with your life, and I want the world to know just how cool you are.

I can't wait until you start posting new pictures. But in the meantime, I look at a lot of the old tagged pictures on my profile. I've found some cool pics, like when we went to prom together, or when we performed at our first talent show, or when we went panning for gold in Old Town. So many great memories.

But your name doesn't show up in the tag anymore when I'm looking on my profile, 'cuz you blocked me. I just see a black box with white letters that doesn't link to any profile.

It's like you're not even there anymore.

You're there, but you're not.

One of my favorite pics someone tagged us in is from the elementary school talent show. I think they posted it after I won. You got so nervous and almost freaked out when the microphone started feeding back. I remember it like it was yesterday. Maybe you can thank all of those Throwback Thursdays or Flashback Fridays for those more embarrassing moments. The internet never forgets, but hopefully it forgives.

It's amazing, the memories we can access at our fingertips, all thanks to social media. Even so, I definitely gotta gift you a picture album sometime in the future, once we start talking again, because it's still fun to hold the real thing in your hands.

Erica, these pictures—these memories—mean everything to me.

I know they say a picture is worth a thousand words, but all the platitudes and clichés exist for a reason. When I look at them, they truly take me back to the very moment we shared those experiences together.

And it kills me.

It kills me not knowing what you're up to. It's so hard. And it kills me that I can't even text you anymore without hearing back. I mean, I know you didn't straight up tell me to not reach out to you, so it's not like we're on extremely bad terms or anything, but where does that leave us? You're not ghosting me, but I don't want to keep playing Russian Roulette with you. I'm afraid that if I send one more message, it might completely destroy our relationship forever.

I know we're not talking right now, and I know we have our…differences…when it comes to the world of Hollywood, of partying, but I really do appreciate you looking after me. I know I went a little too hard the last time we hung out. I didn't mean to. I think I just underestimated my own tolerance. Isn't it funny, that I'm your big sister, and you're my younger, and you're the one who's supposed to get into trouble, not me?

It must have been difficult to see me like that for the first time. It really is weird to see something taboo get a little out of hand. I swear, though, it was just a one-time thing, and it's a thing of the past and it's a thing I am not super proud of. Regardless, I understand why you're keeping your distance, at least for the time being, because you're trying your hardest, too.

I mean, I tried driving Lyft and Uber once for that weekend after you helped sign me up, and people treated me so badly I wanted to cry. People can be so freaking rude. I think that's what made me want to audition for *The Anthem* in the first place. I wanted to prove something to those people.

Like you always say, you can tell a lot about a person by the way they treat their waitress…or their Lyft driver.

I'm so proud of all that you're accomplishing. You really are one of the hardest workers I know. I swear, once my album goes gold, and if, or when, I become a millionaire, I will pay off any single debt you want, if you'll let me.

I hope that doesn't sound arrogant. I just want you to know that you're worth more than your weight in gold to me. I do love you, my Er-Bear.

So…with all of that being said, can I share a few things with you? But only if I trim out the weird stuff. Or maybe I can just leave it in. It'll be more exciting that way. I'll give you a little bit of that raw, vulnerable, sex, drugs, and rock n' roll part of me, if you're okay with that.

So, here goes.

Today's show was literally unbelievable. The audience roared as we started the finale, a melody of the top 40 hits we had performed on our season of *The Anthem*. They told us that apparently the first season was so successful that every show sold out within the first hour. They're already in talks about a second tour, which would be a year out from now. Isn't that cool?

The producers said that the entire team has finally "made it," whatever *it* is, and all we have to do is our *thing*, whatever our *thing* is. That's what everyone kept saying. We already made it through the ranks of what technically could be called a game show, and here we are, the winners. There's nothing left for us to fear. We made it through the worst of the auditions and the excruciating hours of taping the season, and now all we need to do is enjoy ourselves. The only thing we need to do from here on out?

Survive.

Easy enough, right?

The speakers shook the walls of the 10,000-seat amphitheater as the band crescendoed, swelling into the last movement of a song. The pyrotechnic sparklers twirled behind us, sparks flying in electric pinwheels, brilliant lights shooting through the dense fog. We burst into lush, ten-part harmony, a sweet polyphonic cadence before our last note. We've been practicing in rehearsals for the better half of two months, and even though I'm so familiar with the song that I could sing it in my sleep, we sang with so much energy that I couldn't help but burst into tears.

I got overwhelmed because I started thinking of you.

I looked out through the spotlight and the falling technicolor confetti. It was everything I've dreamed of, everything I've ever longed for.

It would've been perfect.

But only one person was missing.

You.

It was so strange. I knew you weren't here tonight, but I still tried searching for you through the blazing lights, scanning the endless crowd of raving *Anthem* fans, hoping to see you, even for a moment.

Maybe you were in the nosebleeds, or maybe you were watching me from the livestream at home, celebrating me from a screen away. I could've sworn I heard your voice, saying my name from afar.

As the lights went out, and the spotlight faded around me, the room grew dark. In the plastic barrier in front of the soundboard, I saw your reflection there.

When I blinked, I swore, Erica, you were there, smiling at me, floating somewhere in that brief flash of darkness when the world becomes full of possibilities.

Like a ghost, you were there.

You always would be.

It shocked me. I had never felt so many butterflies floating around in my stomach.

Erica, were you here tonight?

But as I opened my eyes, something else was in your place.

What I thought was you became something else. It was like my own reflection merging with yours. Your smile faded away as a dark shadow hovered over it, encompassing you in a shining pool of shadowy light, morphing the corners of your lips into a sneer.

A figure stood there, right where you were, front row and center, its body as transparent as the fog hanging over the crowd, its smile like a scar. It was an amalgamation of shadows and sunlight and the glitter that fills the ocean when the sun shines at just the right angle, infinite starlight playing upon the tide pools, creatures unaware of their physical presence causing their own shadows.

And then I knew.

I knew exactly what it was.

It was that thing you saw in the mirror back when we were kids. The shadows, the ectoplasm that you told me about, the ever-shifting shadowy sunlight.

A sudden dread filled me. I hadn't believed you. And you probably still hate me for it, too.

As I stood on the stage, you began to reveal yourself to me in different fractals. In that brief flash of darkness, the shadows started reaching out toward me. I could feel them pulling me into another place. I didn't see it then, but I see it now, typing this, if you know what I mean.

What I had tried so hard to run away from finally came back to haunt me.

You were there, and you weren't.

This shadow, this light, *knew* you hated me.

And then I heard you say my name.

The ectoplasm began to fade away.

You were watching over me, weren't you? Somewhere, within my heart, you were still there, making the monsters go away, like I had done for you when you fell into the mirror and became trapped there.

Are you still there, on the other side of that mirror?

As the entity dissolved into the darkness, I missed my cue and rolled onto my ankle. A searing pain shot through my leg as I tried to lift myself up. I cursed at myself for giving in to the fear.

I wish it had been you. Maybe then I wouldn't be hurting.

That's the thing about ghosts.

They're always there, waiting in the shadows for your guard to fall.

-Dianne

Chapter Eleven

As I finished reading Dianne's message, the sky began to fall.

In the center of the Interstate, the horizon alit in wondrous, cosmic colors like a newborn nebula, its memories shooting out like lightning, branching from its core in relentless tornadoes. It pushed the boundaries of everything in sight, cascading through the endless void. My vantage point disappeared entirely, and I soon found myself suspended in time, floating in a wild burst of neon energy, fueled by the memories of the universe.

I tumbled through the looking glass, flying in that place in the sky where memories go to die.

My life flashed before my eyes.

That's when the neuroflash started.

The colors dripped onto my skin, morphing into a rainbow ectoplasm that slithered across me, spiraling in successive vortexes like a guided missile. The light burrowed under my skin and slid between my bones, dancing through my heart until it twirled across my mind. It glided through my veins in a supercharged rush of adrenaline, empowering me with the flash of memories I had seen long ago, when I had fallen through to the other side of this mirror.

My head began resonating with a soft, high-pitched frequency, panning from left to right, surrounding me until it glimmered across my skull. It was the sound of infinite memories swirling through my brain. The sound of dead, *forgotten memories being remembered. The sound of a newborn star remembering it had been born once before.*

My life flashed over and over again until the world around me dissolved entirely.

~ ~ ~

I took a deep breath and grounded myself. I had been floating for so long that I didn't know which way was up. I was standing in front of a computer now. In the screen, Macy's transparent smile faded as she disappeared through the looking glass.

In the mirror, I saw my reflection. I gasped. I couldn't believe my eyes. I had never noticed my jaw literally drop like that before.

"Erica, are you okay?"

Someone tapped on my shoulder. It was in the rhythm of *two nickels and a dime*, seven taps in brief succession, the way she always knocked wherever she went. Whether it was at home, or knocking on our bedroom door, or honking her car horn when she wanted to prank me from across the driveway.

It was her. She was living, breathing, alive.

"Dianne."

For a moment I could only stand there, breathless, stunned by her presence.

I reached out and grabbed her hand. The warmth of her skin filled the endless coldness I had experienced in that void, within the Interstate, in the nothingness between the stars. This time, my fingers didn't go through hers, like they had with Macy's. I never knew warmth could have an identifying quality about it, like a fingerprint, but it was hers. She had come back to life.

"Hey, you little stinker, snap out of it!" She placed her hands on my shoulders and playfully shook me. We stood in an empty classroom at

Bryworld Elementary School. She was eleven, her classic rainbow braces painting her smile with a metallic finish. She had glittery makeup on her cheeks, the same kind I remembered seeing in a Throwback Thursday someone had posted on my timeline a few months ago. "Come on, you silly goose. Who else *would* I be?"

It hit me where we were, what day this was. We were about to perform at our first elementary school talent show. My hands grew clammy at the thought. I had screwed it up back then, and now, I had to relive that moment in real time.

"It's really you." I was so happy I almost cried. I gave her the biggest bear-hug I could. "I thought I'd never see you again."

"Jeez, Erica. I've only been gone for like, maybe a minute or so? Are you okay? You nervous or something?"

I shook my head. "Nervous? Me? No. Come on, I'm never nervous."

"Okay, whatever you say. We've got like, hmmm, maybe ten minutes 'til we're on."

"Oh yeah, for the talent show!"

"My god. You got the weirdest pre-show butterflies, don't you? Whatever you need to do, just do it, 'cuz it's showtime, baby!"

She wiggled her fingers in a jazz-hands fashion and proceeded to do her regular vocal warmups. We sang in harmony, ascending through a few different scales, spontaneously changing keys according to her heart's desires. Then, she switched into the glottal explosion part of her exercises, where she sang from the lowest part of her register to the highest, imitating the sound of a nasally siren, ascending and descending in shimmering, slightly off-key soundwave waterfalls. It was shrill and piercing and even a little annoying, but it filled me with so much happiness to hear her again that I probably could have listened to it all day.

It was so strange to experience this memory knowing that I was reliving it in the present. I was possessed with a new awareness of free will that I had never experienced before. It was as though that *deja-vu* part of my brain propelled me to speak and move in certain ways, like performing choreography I never knew I had learned. I hit the marks right on cue.

"You ready for this?" I gave her a gentle nudge on her arm. "You ready to show the world what you got, Miss *Westfieeeeeld of Southern Cal-i-for-ni-a*?"

"Born ready," she said, nodding. "Since the day little Miss Dianne was a wee little baby, since the moment she started saying *Momma* and *Dadda*, she has been preparing for this very moment, when she and her sister will show the world what they've got. How about you, my Er-bear? Were you born ready, too?"

"Oh, you know it. It's game time. Let's get ready to rock n' roll!"

She placed her arm around my shoulder, and we walked out the way we always would, together, eager to learn what waited for us there, in the future.

From the middle of the room, the emcee, Mrs. Garmain, began to speak in front of the curtain. We took our places behind the microphone.

"Very good, very good. Go ahead and give them another round of applause. Yes, great, great job. Okay. And now, next, we have none other than the world-famous sister duo to close off the night, none other than Dianne and Erica Westfield!"

The audience roared as Mrs. Garmain gave the go-ahead to the sound guy at the end of the room to start playing our instrumental music track. It was the beginning of a song from the musical *Les Mis*, a melancholic violin that swelled into an orchestral underscore.

Then, the curtain swung open, and we stood in front of the entire school. I couldn't remember myself panicking back then, but now, the future stretched out before me. I couldn't reveal that I knew what was there on the other side of this song.

We started singing at the top of our lungs. This was our moment to shine. Although I hadn't seen the musical in years, I remembered the words perfectly. The audience was entranced as we crescendoed into the chorus. Now, I had to sing a harmony to help boost Dianne up.

But at the end of the auditorium, I saw something that made my stomach drop.

Those shadows, that neon light, the same one I saw in class just a few weeks prior, glowing from behind a screen. It manifested near the soundboard's computer monitor, catapulting into the spotlight that shone on us.

"No." I wrapped my hands around my ears. Dianne shot me a look. I stood so close to the microphone that it caused a burst of feedback. A few laughs pealed through the audience from our fellow classmates, and my cheeks flushed in embarrassment. When this happened the first time, I didn't know why I felt so odd in this moment, but I had a feeling. "No no no no no."

I closed my eyes so hard there wasn't any trace of light. For a moment I was lost in the darkness. I opened my eyes again, but no matter how hard I tried, it didn't make the monsters go away.

I looked at Dianne's eyes, but the shadows were not reflecting in hers.

It had to be me, then. I needed to face my fears in order to protect the memories of the future from possessing her.

A static white noise came from the computer speakers. Some people turned around and then immediately looked back to us, unaware of the evils that buzzed to life within. But they didn't know what was happening.

Bloody Mary was hacking my memories.

And then I heard a voice, almost inaudible, until it finally crystallized into words. It was dowsed in reverb, as though it were funneled through a large tunnel at the other side of the universe, from the other side of her mirror, where she was speaking to me now.

"You were always jealous, weren't you, Erica? Even back then, here, now, you knew she would be in the spotlight forever, and you would only be left in the shadows, cold, alone, until the day you died. You didn't know how right you were back then."

The lights dimmed. I spoke to Bloody Mary's voice, from behind this side of my mirror. "That's not true. The spotlight was big enough for both of us. Just because she was the center of attention didn't mean I wasn't happy for her. Let me just enjoy this moment again."

"But you weren't, as you have seen on the other side, when you did not go to her debut show as an international superstar. You and I both know that is a lie, and you have only been kidding yourself for years."

"Stop saying that. You don't know what I've been through."

"Oh, but I do. I have seen everything, Erica. I have seen your dreams; I have fed off your memories. And now, I am here in this memory that is not a memory. Look at you. Look at how pathetic you were. Here you are, performing your very first show, and you let the shadows of the future trap you in this moment. It looks like someone had a little case of stage fright, didn't they?"

"It doesn't matter what anyone else thinks…or thought, I mean. Stop doing this to me. I just want to enjoy singing with her while it still lasts. I will protect her from you."

"You didn't really protect her, though. You didn't even know how to tie your own shoes, let alone stop her from dying. Don't fool yourself into thinking you were stronger than you actually were. No, child. You are just buying time that you do not have."

"You're wrong," I said through clenched teeth. "I did everything I could to protect her, even if she didn't know it at the time."

"You were supportive, yes, until you weren't. You were enabling her in ways you never knew. You didn't even know just how deeply she would fall. Now, you must pay the price for falling back into this moment, or I will make Dianne remember what waits for her—there, in the future, now, in the past. Maybe I will even freeze her in this moment so she will never know what waits for her on the other side of these memories."

"No. I won't let you do that." I felt the power of the neuroflash resonating within my skull. I could control it now, the velocity of the memories, the way they materialized in front of me like a manic social media profile's timeline, status updates flying across my mind until they dripped from my fingers in a soft burst of light. "Not now, not then."

"Ah. Very good, Erica. You are growing stronger. You are remembering the power I gave to you."

I looked down at my hands. Ectoplasm swirled from my fingertips. A rush of static electricity shot through my arms. It was like walking on a foot that had fallen asleep. I could feel part of my body there, but it was inactive, a phantom limb, waiting to come back to life. The starlight had been within my heart, all along.

"Don't make me do this, not here, when I need to finish this song. Let me live in this moment."

"We shall see if you do, then." The static noise coming through the sound system increased in amplitude. Her voice grew two octaves deeper. "My reflections will transcend through the mirror."

Ectoplasm bolted out of the computer monitor on the other side of the auditorium like the tentacles of a giant kraken, unleashed from the bottomless blue by Bloody Mary herself. The ground wobbled and shook until it fell from beneath me, and then I was hovering, gliding through the murky waters in the deepest trenches within the seven seas.

I held my ground as the Bloody Mary's crimson ectoplasm eclipsed everything in sight. Sparks shot out of my fingertips as I stood there, flying but sinking, almost motionless but moving through infinity. I needed to protect Dianne. I couldn't let anything bad happen to her. If she learned how she would die, then she would never finish the song. She would never pursue her dreams. I needed to do something, now.

I dashed through the technicolor light, dissolving it with my own ectoplasm until they peeled back like tar. I was terrified at what was hovering around me, of what these memories contained.

As I walked through the auditorium, the ghosts of my past danced in my peripheral. I could hear them now, tempting me to find them. I walked through the open door to the outdoor cafeteria, which was revealed to me through the soft starlight above. There was something in the way the light fell onto the ground that made everything appear suspended in time. Maybe those were the same stars Macy had seen. Maybe in this time, here in the Interstate, they were still not dead stars; they had always been shining there, in that infinite moment, waiting to help me fight off the ghosts.

At the other end of the cafeteria, the ectoplasm crystallized into a form. It was a distorted reflection of Bloody Mary, one of the ghosts that had once walked with her, years ago. Though I made no sound, gliding across the earth, the ghost must've felt the static of the ectoplasm churning through my veins.

"Well, well, well. Look who finally decided to show up again." It was a man's voice, but it was Bloody Mary's, too. I could tell he was just pretending. He wasn't human. He was a distorted reflection of everyone who had lived before him. "I've been waiting here for quite some time, you know."

He turned slowly, the moonlight shining through his transparent body.

He smiled, his lips stretching out like a deep rift in the Earth. It was tectonic, the collision of the corners of his lips, revealing endless tree roots and shadow hands that slithered in his mouth like insects. He was a dead man walking. While looking at him, I felt as though I was staring through the planet straight to its core, and all of the death it contained, culminating into a sick recreation of life with all of the dead memories that had waited there, in the space between the stars, where I now found myself.

"You shouldn't have waited so long," I said. I thought about what Macy had told me, how she couldn't remember how she died. Maybe this shadow didn't know how long I'd been floating here, either. Maybe he was just as afraid as I was. I had transformed into something like a ghost, after all. I needed to do my best to play the part. "Now go back into the mirror, where you belong."

"Bloody Mary's memories are not forgotten that easily." He put his hands on his hips, reaching for something. "Tell us, Erica. Why should Dianne be set free?"

He lifted into the air, soaring over the cafeteria tables, propelled by the dead starlight shining through his dead body. Ectoplasm dripped from his skin in lush waves of eternal sunlight, leaving a long, glittering wake behind him.

I ducked beneath one of the tables. I needed to find a way to make this evil reflection of Bloody Mary disappear. I was defenseless to the weight of her memories.

But I, too, was possessed with memories, and maybe I stood a chance against the infinite void contained in Bloody Mary's eyes.

I looked at my hands, desperate to channel the same power of starlight that Bloody Mary's reflection had propelled through his skin. I urged myself to neuroflash, to channel the true strength of the ectoplasm from my veins. But they were dim, only mere bolts of static light. I needed to learn how to truly shine from within.

"Come out, come out wherever you are." Bloody Mary's voice bounced between the tables, between the handball courts, where Dianne and I had become handball champions just days ago, years ago, in the Interstate. "You can't hide from us. We'll always find you, in the end."

I crawled through the rusty, metallic pipes underneath the tables, nearly hitting my head. I held my breath and contained the light surrounding me. I reached the cement wall that marked the end of the tables. Pressing my back against the cement, I sidled against the wall and searched through the starlight, scanning the shadows for even the faintest movement.

At last, I saw him there, sitting, munching on an apple that had been tossed into the trashcan decades ago. I aimed my fingers at him, preparing the ectoplasm to burst out into bolts.

He turned and looked my way, smiling again. "There you are! Yummy stuff, ain't it, the food humans create. Mind if I feed off your memories for a little bit? That way I won't go hungry for another few eternities!"

"Never!" I shouted. "Stop hacking my memories!"

"I'm afraid we don't have a choice. Once we've fallen through the mirror, all we have left is our memories, until they die, too. You don't remember this one, do you?"

"No, because I'm living it now."

"Well then, I'll show you how it ends."

He launched into the air again, rushing toward me.

I channeled the neuroflash, the ectoplasm flashing from my fingertips, elongating into giant tendrils of electromagnetic air particles, swirling and shifting with the power of the dead starlight that shone over us.

I catapulted into the air, propelled by the memories from the future. I was a shooting star, swirling through the shadows, making sense of my newfound gravity. In the void, the man laughed, echoing through the shadows and the visions they had hidden long ago.

"Do you really think you stand a chance against Bloody Mary?" The man glided toward me and stopped in place, hovering over the middle of the cafeteria. "Do you think you can travel through the other end of her mirror?"

Ectoplasm churned through my veins. I was prepared to destroy him. The weight of the universe pressed down on me, but I would not let it stop me. "I'll do anything for Dianne."

"And what makes you think that changes things, girl?"

"Because I will stand by my sister, at least for now, here, in this moment, and together, we can do anything."

"My, my. What a very sweet thing to say. Except, your sister isn't here now, is she? She's already dead, and you're just pretending that she's still alive. So, why not become a reflection, like us, and help Bloody Mary catalogue the memories of the universe? Then you can do this all the time, fly through infinity."

"I'd rather die and have my memories eaten up by the stars if that means Dianne would be forgotten."

I was shimmering now.

I raised my arms into the sky and thought of the future, of those happy moments with Dianne that waited for me somewhere in the near present. I channeled the memories that transcended through to the other side of the looking glass and felt them sparkle in my blood.

The man's empty eyes widened. For a moment he almost looked afraid.

"Are you scared?" I said, feeling the starlight glimmering through my voice. "I thought you were already dead. I thought these things didn't matter anymore."

He opened his mouth to speak. He only hovered there, terrified of my light and the stars that shone through me.

"I'll see you on the other side of the mirror, then."

Starlight burst from my core. The neuroflash imploded within me like a supernova. I became something like dead starlight. Ectoplasm shot through my fingertips and pierced through his spirit.

He hissed as he dissolved into a crimson pool of ectoplasm at the center of the cafeteria. I tried picking it up, to feel what these dead memories contained, but it only faded through my fingertips.

I ran back through the doors of the auditorium, back to the talent show, and took my place on stage. The light around my body dimmed, and I became human again, back in the same memory. I had defeated the memories of the future from hacking into this moment. But Dianne would never know that. She just thought I froze and had stage fright.

Opening my mouth, I sang my heart out despite the trembling of my nerves and the dread filling my stomach and the ghosts I had just battled. I was filled with joy as we reached the last phrase.

A pin-drop silence filled the room.

The entire audience broke out into applause. Some people jumped to their feet in a standing ovation. When we left the stage, we ran up to our parents and hugged them, and they gave us bags of candy, those blue raspberry sour belts we had always loved.

They could tell I was down on myself. But I couldn't tell them what had happened. No one would believe me.

"Don't worry about it, sweetheart. You guys did such an amazing job, wow!" Mom leaned in and offered me a kiss on the cheek. "You two are rock stars!"

"Terrific," Dad said, patting me on the back. "Absolutely outstanding. I am so proud of you!"

"Erica, what happened?" Dianne crossed her arms. She couldn't even look me in the eyes. "You made me mess up."

"I'm sorry, I didn't mean to—"

"I told you to stand at least a few inches from the mic so it doesn't feed back."

"Hey," Mom said, leaning into Dianne's ear. "Now is *not the time*. You guys did great. Just let it go"

"Erica, *come on*."

"I'm sorry, it's not my fault! I promise!"

That feeling, that helplessness, grew in the pit of my stomach. And then, an instant jealousy emerged, as Mrs. Garmain came over and showered Dianne with attention.

"Wow, you were both so amazing. But…Dianne, wow, just wow. I didn't know you can sing that high!"

Dianne brushed her hair behind her ears and looked bashfully down. "I really appreciate you saying that."

In my head, I heard my past self mimicking the way she said this, so obviously feigning humbleness that it made me sick. Maybe it was the first glimmer of jealousness I had ever felt. It was enough to send butterflies through my stomach, their wings like razors, slashing my insides apart. If Mary hadn't stopped me from shining, then we would both be shining starlets.

Tears pooled at the corners of my eyes, and I tried my hardest to keep them contained, but then I blinked and they started falling. My makeup streamed down my face, creating ugly rivers of eyeliner at the corners of my chin. The precious aftermath of our first performance was destroyed. But at least I had saved Dianne.

"Hey, Erica, I'm sorry," Dianne said, but I wasn't really listening, because at the other end of the room, I saw the shadows of Mary's reflection dissolving back into the computer monitor. I hadn't stopped them completely. They were going somewhere else. I needed to travel with them, so I wouldn't become trapped in this memory.

I ran to the computer and buried my head near the screen, prepared to neuroflash into the future. I hoped I just appeared to be to hiding myself from crying in front of everyone else. I hoped they thought I was just having a moment to process my emotions. But what they didn't know was, this would be the last time I would see them like this, and as much as I wanted to say goodbye, I couldn't, because it would reveal the knowledge of the stars and the terrors that waited for us there, in the future.

My mind neuroflashed through the screen, and I started drifting there, in the infinite place where memories go to die.

CHAPTER TWELVE

That night, Erica, I became possessed.

In the locket, the ectoplasm was no longer reflecting onto me but through me. I had become something like a ghost, suspended in that place between the stars, my body physically transforming as my mind drifted into infinity. The reflection of the universe melted from the sky straight into my soul, and soon the cosmos spun within my heart, whispering to me its ancient secrets.

I heard the memories of the dead calling to me from the place where memories go to die, where they had been waiting for me to reflect their ancient knowledge through the looking glass. They revealed to me the power of the starlight, the sheer magnitude of immortality. It wasn't my life that flashed before my eyes—it was the endless birth and death cycles of the planets, the rebirth of the universe, unfurling before my mind like flower petals, sweet, intuitive, and enchanting.

Soon, I was able to propel the starlight through my fingertips, channeling its infinite energy to revive those who had succumbed to the cold of the Oregon Trail. Perhaps I would really have a chance to see my parents again. Maybe I would even be able to bring them back to life, if I was lucky enough to remember where they had died.

Something within me is shifting, still. I do not think it is a coincidence our paths have crossed. It is allowing us to re-experience these moments together, with a new perspective, even if we are two social media timelines apart, traveling through the same shadows between both sides of our mirrors. Our memories seem to be merging together. We must do anything we can to help keep these memories from being rewritten, or destroyed.

After my parents died, I was never really alone in my journey, was I? I had you. It should come as no surprise to you, then, Erica, that the same voice that spoke to me from above was the same voice you just heard in your memories. It was Mary all along. However, at the time, I did not know that, for the voice had not been distorted through the echo chamber of our memories.

Back then, it was a benevolent spirit, speaking to me from beyond, encouraging me to withstand the cold. She soon grew manipulative, cunning, evil, as our memories will soon reveal to us. What she didn't know was that you and I were linked through the stars, our destinies prewritten in the constellations. We actually still have a chance to reflect that light back into Bloody Mary's eyes, if she is even capable of remembering.

That night, as my reflection morphed before my very eyes, I had a choice to make. I could either become afraid of what was happening to me, or I could explore its power, possibly use it for good. I could either become hateful and resentful, running away from the pain of my parents' death, or I could run toward something else—a brighter future, maybe even making it through to the other side of the trail, to California, to fulfill my parents' last wishes.

After wandering alone for so long, I finally had a new sense of direction, the ectoplasm guiding me through the shadows. So, I rode through the darkness, equipped with this new sense of light, Bessie pulling me through the wintry storm, determined to utilize the power of the stars to help those who had fallen on the trail.

One night, though, as I followed the sparks of electricity shooting through my fingertips, alighting the path before me, I arrived at an abandoned encampment. It looked all too familiar. I had a feeling in the pit of my stomach that I couldn't quite place my finger on. Something in the air wasn't quite right. I had seen a lot of death back then, traveling with my own caravan, so I already had an idea about what waited for me there, in the shadows. With this new light, however, perhaps there was nothing to fear anymore. So, I hopped off Bessie and walked slowly into the darkness beyond.

It was a bloodbath. The smell of rot and decay trailed through the air. Though I had become accustomed to death, I couldn't process the amount of life that had been destroyed there. Bodies lay half-frozen in the snow, surrounding a fire pit that was still burning, its embers nearly fading to ash. Crimson gore covered the snow around them. They had died recently, I knew that much, barely frozen in the arctic winds, blood pooling through the bullet holes that pierced through their flesh. But who had killed them, and why?

As I walked forth, the ectoplasm shot through the shadows, revealing the corpses in full technicolor. The sights tore through my heart. They were families, Erica. Children. Grandparents. They were not outlaws or bandits. There were mothers and fathers and sisters and brothers and friends and neighbors who had left everything behind them to pursue a better future. They had already traveled this far on the trail, and yet, here they were, dead, just like my family.

I had never felt an immediate sense of grief in my life before, but I started crying, sobbing, weeping. I had only fooled myself into thinking that I was okay. I still thought that maybe, just maybe, I'd have a chance to bring my parents back to life, but I realized right then and there that I would never find them. They were already fading to dust in the darkness, like dead stars. But these bodies I came across still had a chance to be awoken. Lying in the snow, helpless to the wounds that had destroyed them, unaware of how quickly their lives had changed, these people did not deserve to be forgotten.

As I cried, the ectoplasm merged with my tears. The memories of the universe fell through my eyes, dripping through to the snow and the lifeless bodies around me. If there was any cosmic purpose to this destruction, some long-forgotten meaning to the desecration of humanity and the power of evil, then it needed to be revealed to me, through the memories trapped in this ectoplasm. Otherwise, life would have been for nothing. There would be no sense going on any further if in the end we would all just lay there, dead.

Was anything really waiting for us there, on the other side?

And then I saw something. It was so extraordinary that I couldn't believe my eyes. The light, Erica, the ectoplasm that you and I both possess, it hovered from my tears and my fingertips into the snow, into the bodies, into the precious life that had been destroyed.

Something in the earth began resonating, like an ancient key unlocking some long-forgotten gate, turning, creaking, like starlight dripping onto the ground.

Time seemed to move in reverse, as if an hourglass had been flipped on its head and everything traveled backwards with it. The light dried up the blood and the gore and the rotting flesh. It spiraled through the air like miniature shooting stars, filling their festering bullet holes with light, cauterizing their wounds. The more I focused in on that feeling of grief, of the mysteries of life and death, of good and evil, the brighter I burned, and the quicker they healed. I allowed it to move through me, this feeling, supplied by the memories that waited for us above.

I brought them back to life.

I stood before a deceased woman cradling a frozen child, staring lifelessly into the sky. I couldn't fathom the pain they must have experienced, dying together, in the middle of nowhere, helpless to the shadows that had destroyed them. I couldn't let them fade away.

I waved my hand over her body, light dripping from my skin like a gentle rain. The ectoplasm merged into her skin, crystallizing into her veins. It swirled up to her eyes—the windows of her soul—casting a soft glow within.

She turned to me, unaware of my presence. Her eyes grew full of life, of recognition, as though she had experienced a terrible nightmare and remembered that she was still alive, no longer dreaming, no longer entrapped in that terrible void she had fallen into.

She kissed her child on the forehead. The light trailed from her hand to her child's, like stars collecting into a constellation. They were alive again.

The child stirred from her slumber and sat up. She looked deeply into her mother's eyes, processing her surroundings. She, too, had fallen into a place of terror.

"Mother?" the girl asked. She turned around but did not notice I had been standing there. It almost looked as though she stared straight through me. Perhaps I had transformed into something like a ghost to them. "What happened?"

"Are you all right?"

"I had a dream that I could not wake, and when I awoke, I realized I had not been dreaming."

"We were saved."

"Saved?"

"By angels, watching from above."

"Were we dead, then?"

"No."

I stood there, the universe shining through me, wondering just what to say.

They didn't know why they were so surprised to be waking up. They had done the same so many times before, here on the trail. This reawakening, however, was clearly different, and their mortal brains couldn't wrap around it. Although their spirits had been broken, their bodies had another chance at life. Something within the starlight had granted them the strength to transcend from the dead and return to their journey through the most perilous winter they had ever experienced.

"Were you dreaming, Mother?"

"No."

"Then we were asleep?"

"Please, quiet your voice. You do not want to wake the others."

"Are they coming, too?"

They looked back. The mother shrugged. "We will know soon."

The others were shifting in their sleep, too, as though reaching the end of a nightmare. I had brought them back to life. I had transferred some cosmic energy from the stars straight into their blood, just as it had reflected into me, though the looking glass. I had granted them the source power that was given to us as the universe was created by the hands of some unseen author. The same energy that was contained in the sky was now trailing through them, and if you looked at them, you would never have known that they had just returned from death.

As the mother helped her child stand, they both looked at me. I believe they noticed me as they would perceive the reflection of a distant star. They didn't see me but saw through me. I was a ghost, dancing in their peripheral, a guardian angel that had restored them with the breath of life.

"If we were not asleep, then where were we, Mother?"

"Daydreaming."

"But it is nighttime."

I stood there, seen but not seen, watching as the mother and daughter, reborn with the new light, prepared to descend into darkness.

"We do not know where we were, but soon, we will travel toward where we need to be. Let us remember that the stars have shone tonight."

As I watched them disappear into the night, along with the rest of their caravan, I realized that I had discovered what I was looking for, too.

The way back.

They were traveling in a rush of gold, and I was rushing toward the dead, so I needed to keep going there, in the opposite direction, away from life and any signs of civilization to help bring light to those who had fallen in the harshest reaches of the desolate tundra. That way, I would find them. Eventually, I would relocate where my parents had been murdered. I needed to bring them back to life, because I grew worried that one day, perhaps the stars would stop shining, and I might lose that power. Perhaps one day, when I searched into the night sky, the stars would be dead, too.

So, I began retracing my steps. Maybe it would be soon, maybe it would be years from now, but I would find them again, no matter what. Though everyone was traveling one way, I was traveling the other. Slowly but surely, I found myself encountering many different encampments that had been claimed by unspeakable atrocities, like cannibalism or murder or death or starvation. Really, though, I knew what had driven these people to desperation. It was the evil that waited in the shadows, those evil men who had killed my parents, entrancing them with the reflection of the dead starlight, trapping their memories in this trail forever.

Death remained the only constant, as I traveled backwards, toward that last second of life I shared with my parents. Every wicked way of dying became revealed to me, and I expelled this cosmic ectoplasm onto the dead carcasses that needed to remember the quality of light that life contained.

But, unlike the skies, I was finite. I was losing strength. I was just a vessel of this infinity that I floated in. Every night, after I would raise souls back from the dead, I needed to recharge my energy. To resupply my body with the starlight, I needed to look deeper into the mirror and transfer the stars from the sky to my heart. I remained diligent, never missing a night sky. If I did miss a night, however, then I would start to grow cold. So, I remained faithful to the mirror, to the memories it contained, and I wouldn't stop for anything.

I rode on, possessed with the power of starlight, pushing ever onward through the infinite darkness, until one day, I fell into a trap.

CHAPTER THIRTEEN

DIANNE

Hey Erica,

I know that things happen for a reason, and I'd like a real reason to believe that, but to be honest, I'm not so sure anymore.

And I don't mean that in a "I'm losing hope" kind of way. It just seems like there's no rhyme or reason to some of the darker things that happen in life. It wasn't my fault that I sprained my ankle on the first night of my tour, but it was my fault that I ended up doing what I did. I have to be responsible for my own actions, and their consequences.

I let myself get distracted.

When those shadows tried reaching for me tonight, Erica, it was truly terrifying. It made me think of all those times you told me about them, how the shadows would follow you and make you forget about the light. I didn't not believe you back then, which sounds redundant, but it's true. You never fully realize what someone's going through until you experience it yourself. I never would've tripped and stumbled if it didn't bring back the memories of our childhood.

For some reason, it made me think of all those times when you would wake me up at night, climbing up the ladder to the top of the bunk bed, shaking my shoulder until I awoke. You were afraid of what might happen to you when you woke up in the darkness. You had a big imagination, and your dreams were always merging with reality. You were always fine falling asleep with the lights on, but you insisted that you would not want to wake back up until morning. If you did, you would scream, and I would turn the lights on to show you there were no monsters waiting in the darkness. Nothing was coming out of the mirror, not anymore at least. You were easily spooked.

And I don't mean that in a bad way. I know we've talked about some of the things you saw when you looked in the mirror that day, but I think it was more than that. I think you were afraid of the dark, of the things you couldn't see, of the things that had existed before us, long before. I remember this because Mom even made you that monster spray when she put those rose petals, water, and kisses into an empty Windex bottle, conjuring up a potion so you could ward off the monsters when you were alone in our room. Every kid is afraid of the unknown, especially when they're little, when the mysteries of adulthood lie ahead.

But I was thinking of those things when I saw those shadows tonight, the same ones you saw at our talent show. I'm mad at myself because I remember I was so mad at you for fudging up the first chorus of our song. You made me mess up. But I guess you couldn't help it. I'm sorry if I believed you but didn't fully believe you. I did actually believe you, but I also saw monsters when I was a kid, or what I thought were monsters.

Tonight was different.

I felt like I was a kid again, afraid of the dark, of the monsters that I couldn't see.

I ran offstage, limping, hoping to never witness what I saw ever again, to feel that heavy helplessness weighing on my chest.

I needed help.

A throbbing pain shot through my ankle as I steadied myself on the wall, grasping to get a hold of myself, praying that I didn't break my entire leg. If they saw me through the stage wings, I'd be done for—I didn't want any videos going viral. Me, staring at a ghost. They'd put me on medical leave, write off my visitations as delusions, send me home for good.

I couldn't leave so early, not from my first national tour.

"You good, Dianne?"

My tour manager, Kevin Nickel, wrapped his arm around my shoulder, helped me up, and guided me through the stage wings. He was always there for me, ready to catch me when I fell. Maybe it was my own fault; maybe I was a little tipsy and didn't know it. *Lol,* I forgot to add that. I don't mean to leave anything out. This is for you and for your eyes only. I hadn't intended to get tipsy; I'd just forgotten to eat dinner. I didn't want to be bloated. So, before the show, I did a shot in honor of the tour and another shot in honor of you ghosting me online. Could've been both, or neither.

"I want to go back onstage. Just need an ibuprofen or something."

"Take a moment, Dianne. We'll be okay, as long as *you're* okay." Kevin opened the green room door and pushed aside the half-filled beer bottles and beverages covering the table. Some of them crashed to the floor, ice ricocheting off the plastic cups. My eyes watered as I propped my ankle up. "You won't be movin' around so much if you're like this. Just take it easy for a sec, okay?"

Kevin reached into the first-aid kit and took out an elastic brace. Then, he walked to the soda cooler, filled a plastic bag with ice, wrapped it in a towel, and put it on my ankle.

"How long will I have to be here?"

"We'll play it by ear. If you feel better by the finale, then maybe we can have you go onstage. If not, that's totally okay."

"But the show must go on…"

"Your safety comes first, Dianne. The show can find ways to work around it. I'll check up on you in a bit, okay?"

He smiled and closed the door. If there was something I could be grateful for, it was that I knew I could always rely on Kevin, no matter what.

So, I waited. I pretended that I hadn't ended up here because of those shadows covering the walls, those memories that had come rushing toward me. I played it by ear. I drove myself crazy counting down the minutes until I could get back onstage. But part of me didn't even want to go back out there, not if those shadows were waiting for me, too.

What did you see, really, Erica?

What did you see in the mirror when we were kids?

Where did those shadows come from?

On the corner of the wall was a television livestreaming the entire concert, displaying the feed from the front of the house. They were halfway through the show, just before everyone did their solos for the top ten highlight performances. Everything sounded complete, even though I wasn't there. In fact, I even heard my harmony through the speakers, which we had previously recorded on backing tracks, in case of *emergencies.*

Great. On the first night of tour, my situation had turned into some type of an emergency. It was so freaking embarrassing. There I was, having just won the show, and there I sat, not being able to perform said show. It was like some type of cosmic joke. Not that the show was about me, but I was an integral part of the show. I hope that doesn't sound arrogant. I don't mean for it to. That's just what happens when you are ranked from first place to tenth.

After a few minutes, someone knocked on the door.

"Hey, Kev. Think I'm almost ready." I propped myself up and my ankle twisted to the right. A searing pain jolted through my leg. "Okay. Maybe not."

But it was a woman's voice instead.

Francesca's.

She was a second PA, specifically a gopher. Not a marsupial, mind you, haha. Basically, she was the person who said she would "go for" this and got things for us when we wanted them. It felt really cool to have an assistant for the team, but I was careful to only request things when I needed them.

"Knock, knock. Hey. I'm, um, really sorry about what happened out there. Can I come in?"

I was going to say no, but she'd already closed the door behind her. I really didn't like her, to be honest. There was something about her that seemed off. I don't know why. Like she was hiding something. And I know that sounds weird of me to say, when I know we're not talking to each other, but sometimes, you know there's a lot more going on than what's on the surface.

"Isn't your solo coming up soon?"

She looked at my foot and then back to me, holding my gaze for a moment. I got this weird feeling in my stomach, but that was probably the mix of the ibuprofen and the fact that I hadn't eaten anything since lunch. It had been a long day. I'd downed two shots of coconut vodka on an empty stomach, and I regretted partying a little more than I should have. Tour life.

"Looks like that really hurts. Sometimes I get a little sore, too. If you want, I think I have something that could help." I shook my head, but she grabbed her backpack anyways, unzipped the top sleeve, and pulled something out. "You want something a little…stronger?"

She sat next to me and held out a bottle. On the outside, it looked like one of those brandless, over-the-counter type of pain relievers. But it looked a little forged, counterfeit, like a cheap rip-off of the cheap rip-off.

"I mean, um…"

"I flair up a lot. Believe me. I've been on so many tours. So many things can happen. Sometimes I take them just to make it a little easier. You know."

"What is it?"

She held my gaze again, a penetrating stare, searching for something deep within me, although I couldn't tell what, or why. Who was she, really?

Maybe I had been wrong about her. There was something about her eyes that seemed to look through me. I could tell that she used to have a lot of light there, but something had eclipsed it, as though controlled by something else, or someone else, if you wanna get weird.

That's because it *was* weird. I mean, to be completely honest with you again, I had a feeling of what it was, and I kind of already knew what I was getting myself into, but I still did it, anyways. Again, can't really put it into words, but I got one of those feelings when you know you're about to make a wrong turn, and you might be headed down the wrong road for a little while, but you still steer the wheel in that direction, slightly curious as to where you're heading.

You're a Lyft driver, you should know. There are some streets you never knew existed that you just end up on, and you have to keep going through the unpaved street if you want to keep going at all.

"You don't need to go out there, Dianne, not if you're hurting. But I can tell that they really want you there for your last solo. The crowd, I mean, not us. We'll understand regardless."

"So, yeah, I mean, I'm in a lot of pain. It's just so hard. I wish Erica—my sister—were here."

"Aren't you guys from San Diego? She lives right down the street, right?"

"Yeah." I got that weird feeling in my stomach again, and I almost felt like throwing up. I'm sorry to admit this, Erica, but I was sad that you weren't there. And that we weren't talking in general. It's not your fault, though, why I made this decision. Like I said, I know things can change drastically overnight.

"Wow. I'm real sorry to hear that, Dianne." Francesca uncorked the bottle, put a few pills in her hands, and placed one of them on the pink napkin hanging over the table's edge. "That must be hard."

"You have no idea." I felt myself thinking of you again, because I think about you a lot. Well, actually, everything reminds me of you. I can't look at some things and not see you. Does that make sense? And I swore for a moment, out of the corner of my eye, in the green room's mirror, I saw a flash of you.

It was almost like when you accidentally stare at the sun, and you close your eyes, and the image is imprinted into your vision for a millisecond. But in the darkness, you can still see it there, hovering in the horizon, that big bright star of your smile.

"I really miss her."

"Sorry, didn't mean to ask. You don't have to talk about it if you don't want to."

"Thanks. I appreciate it."

"Well, hey. This also takes the edge off, a little."

"Is it gonna screw me up? Is it…um…don't take this the wrong way, but is it legal?"

She laughed. "Oh, please. You don't even know half of the stuff that goes on in Hollyweird. One or two won't hurt you."

I stared at it. I couldn't get sick from stress at the start of the tour, and I couldn't take time off because of a stupid sprain. I just couldn't.

I hope you understand, Erica, why I ended up taking it. It was a combination of things. Not that I'm trying to warn you or give you a PSA about what you should and shouldn't do. I'm just trying to give you perspective about some of the things that have been happening to me.

I shifted on the couch. A pain shot through my ankle again, and I wanted to cry, but Francesca was there and an entire amphitheater of people were out there and I couldn't be a burden to her or to them, too, like I had become a burden to you.

So, I said thanks, sure, I'll have it, and she handed me a fresh glass of water and I took the pill.

-Dianne

CHAPTER FOURTEEN

"Dianne must have had some idea that I was there, behind the mirror in her green room, watching her take her first pill, didn't she, Macy?"

I knew it was true. I thought Dianne had looked at me, because we even locked eyes, but it seemed as though she just stared through me. I had just been standing with her, there at our talent show, and now I was trapped between spaces, in that mirror, looking through those same eyes.

"Macy, if you can hear me, then I would like to make a specific request to please give me a moment back in my apartment at my computer. This is a little too much for me to experience all of this right now.. I need a moment to breathe."

Macy didn't answer.

I was hovering again within that infinite place between the stars, ready to push through to the other side like a fly breaking out of its larvae. It was not a good sensation and it was not necessarily the metamorphosis I had always imagined I'd experience in my late twenties into the beautiful butterfly phase of my early thirties. If thirty was the new twenty, then I'd never crossed the threshold into adulthood, had I? My life was not on track at all.

I neuroflashed into a screen on my phone, which was hooked up to the internet, which must have tapped into the same emotional frequencies as a moment ago, when Dianne was staring at me.

~ ~ ~

I neuroflashed through the rearview mirror in my car and found myself sitting in a parking lot, waiting between Lyft and Uber rides, desperate to make an extra buck for rent. I had already filed a missing person report and she was found and then went to rehab and then she was living back on the streets again. My life was very lopsided. That was the thing about being a gig worker—it had no real stability, and I had no financial buffer to fall back on. I was living paycheck to paycheck, so much so that when the pandemic began, my entire livelihood was ripped out from under me.

And so was Dianne's.

Although she had more of a buffer than me because of her royalties on *Anthem*, she had fallen back into her addiction, and her funds were quickly draining.

It was about 12:14 in the morning. I remembered that number because it felt symmetrical, reflective onto itself. The numbers added up to eight and any of the numbers in that number could be divided by the sum total of its parts. Maybe it was odd that it stood out to me, but perhaps that's what memories do in hindsight—they make even the smallest details appear to have some type of significance.

I had just dropped somebody off at a hotel near downtown San Diego and was on my way to a 7-Eleven to get my next fix of caffeine. I was contemplating buying an energy drink but figured the rush of caffeine might first make me feel tired before I felt recharged again, and I couldn't afford an hour of lethargy, so I settled on buying a coffee cake, Lunchables, and a lightly caffeinated Snapple raspberry black tea. I called it *the works*. It was just enough to keep me going.

I walked out of the 7-Eleven and kept my eyes on the ground, careful not to disturb any of the transients sleeping nearby. It always made me very sad that I could never give them what they needed when they asked for money. I had no extra cash to spare, but I could provide them with a brief hello, a reminder of the humanity that rested on the other side of their coldness.

My stomach rumbled. I was eager to eat my snacks and ready to earn a few extra bucks during the prime-time driving hours between 1 and 3 a.m., when all of the partiers needed a ride back to their apartments. They were all carelessly drunk, stumbling through the streets of downtown San Diego right on 5th Avenue, and it had been my duty to keep them safe.

That specific 7-Eleven shared a parking lot with a Carl's Junior, the one I'd actually go to sometimes when I had drunken nights out with former college friends. It was across from the intersection of the 5 freeway and the 163 North, which provided a triangle of shelter for anyone who wanted to stay out of the rain. I stepped into my car, turned on my app, and was about to embark on the second half of my shift when I heard a voice, muted through the window.

"Excuse me?"

My heart jolted in my chest. Through my rearview mirror, in the drive-thru of the Carl's Jr., Dianne was knocking on car windows, begging for money as people ordered their midnight snacks.

I could tell it was her by her voice, even though she sounded frail and inebriated. I was completely disoriented now—there I was, having just seen Dianne in her youth, at her first show, and here I was, now, possessed with the knowledge of her death. I wondered if I could alter the trajectory of her life, if I just used the right words.

I needed to tread lightly.

"Dianne?"

She turned around, looked up slowly, and tilted her head sideways as if in acknowledgement, nodding diagonally. It was like when an animal suddenly shifted their calm behavior, moving from zero to one hundred, sensing the hidden vibrations in the ground before an earthquake struck. She was ready to flee.

"Thought I heard a voice. Sir, can you spare some change?"

"Dianne, it's *me*." I coasted up to her and rolled down my window. The air smelled of burnt French fries and sewage. It was cold and I could only imagine what she had to endure, here on the endless road. "It's Erica."

"Erica! Oh, hello." She curtsied, clapped her hands, and danced a two-step jig with her feet. "How do you do, thou sister of mine?"

"I should ask you the same."

"*I should ask you the same*," she mimicked, her voice rising two octaves. "Why do you think I'm here? Because I'm hungry. I'm hungry, Erica, real hungry. And sir Carl Junior the third has the best hammies, doesn't he? You got some cash?"

I was tempted to laugh but resisted. Everything about this moment was wrong. Her arm was covered with small, purple bruises and her comatose veins bulged from her arms. She was in another place, and yet, she was right within reach. But she didn't want saving. She just wanted to live her life.

"He's the best cook, isn't he?" I laughed so hard that it echoed through the parking lot, and some of the people in their cars turned around, watching us. "You're so silly, Dianne."

She furrowed her brows and crossed her arms. "I'm *so silly*? That sounds like what you'd say to a kid. We're not kids anymore, Erica."

"I know." Which seemed so strange to me, because just moments ago, I had seen her smiling with her braces still on. "I didn't mean it like that."

"Then why'd you say that to me? I'm an adult. A-D-U-L-T. Say it."

"Because what you said was funny." My voice trembled. "You were always so funny. I love you, I hope you know."

"You too, my sister. You're a fun one, aren't you?" She closed her eyes and her body wobbled, almost as though jerking awake. "Oh, sorry. Nodded off. Dreamt you were here for a sec. Ha. That happens a lot."

"I *am* here."

"But are you, though?"

"Dianne."

"What?"

She wobbled again, almost falling over. She had lost a significant amount of weight, and she was skeletal.

"Do you want a ride?"

She considered this for a moment, then shook her head. "Nah. I'm gonna go eat at Carl's Junior. He's the best cook. You tried his hammies before?"

"Are you cold?"

"A little."

"Then you can come back to my place for a bit if you want. I got a good heater, you know."

"Ah…I'm not that cold. Just a fun night out, is all."

"Please. Dianne. Just get in the car."

"No. You're gonna take me to that place again. Just like you did last time. And then you'll tell me to stay there and that I'm not an adult who is capable of making her own decisions and then I'll be screwed again."

"You have no idea what it took to come back here to see you."

She frowned. "I'm sorry. I'm a burden, aren't I?"

"No. Not at all." I reached out to her. She stepped back. "That's why I'm here, Dianne. Because you're my person. You're never a burden. Please. Just come back home."

"Take me home? Yeah, right. No, you won't. You're just out to get me. Like everyone else."

As I stared into her eyes, I saw something moving there, in the reflection of her dilated pupils.

A figure, hovering over me, shadows forming into the outline of something that had died long ago. That dead starlight, maybe, and the memories they kept suspended in time.

I turned around, but the shadows weren't there. When I looked back, they had already crept up behind her. It was Dianne now who stared into my eyes and saw the reflection of the shadows, of Bloody Mary, stretching her crimson ectoplasm over me.

"No!" Dianne fell onto the ground. She pushed herself away from the car, her hands scratching against the gravel, opening up old wounds. Blood trailed from her fingertips. "Stay back!"

But I couldn't. I wouldn't let the shadows get her, not tonight.

I put my car in park, flashed the hazards on, and jumped out of the car door as the ectoplasm spiraled into the air, coagulating into something like a dark rain cloud around her entire body.

The streetlights faded as darkness eclipsed the sky. We became suspended in time, floating as the world spun around us. Only the faint moonlight from years ago cast its soft glow, shining infinitely through the void.

"Erica, do you remember this moment?" Bloody Mary's voice sounded distorted through my car's speakers. Dianne must've heard her, too, because she looked into the sky, somewhere far past the moon. "You had a lot of money to make, money that you desperately needed, and yet, here you were, fighting for your sister's life, when you already knew she would be dying soon."

"That's not true." I clasped my hands to my ears again. "She needed help."

"Of course, she did. Anyone would know that. But why were you doing this again, when you had already tried intervening so many times before? Did you think this time would be different?"

"You're lying. I wouldn't be here if I couldn't change something."

"That's not how time works here, Erica. And in a parking lot of all places, how very brave of you. And while she pretended to hear you, she wasn't really listening, because she was so high she didn't even know where she was. You were disturbing her, pushing her to her limits. Why did you do this, Erica?"

"I was protecting her."

"Then we shall see if you truly did."

Bloody Mary laughed. Dianne shook her head violently, the laughter drilling into her ears.

"No. Please. Erica, help me."

"Dianne, it's okay." As the ectoplasm spun above her, preparing to unleash their tendrils in a vicious hurricane, I walked toward her, unafraid of the infinite coldness contained in that dead starlight. I would do anything for her. "Just focus on my voice. I'm here with you."

But she was lost, now, too far gone in her drug-fueled hysteria, the chemicals rushing through her veins, the memories of the future dragging her under. She bolted from the ground, running unsteadily as though searching for purchase on a sinking ship, and dashed through the drive-thru.

I ran after her, nearly slipping across the ground as Bloody Mary's ectoplasm crept across the gravel. Their tentacles twirled underneath me like driftwood rushing upstream. They lined either side of us, merging from two dimensions to three, to infinity, sprouting from the floor and twisting into stalactites that elongated into dead oak trees, their gnarled branches clawing at us, pulling us through to the other side.

My body began to burn.

The memories of the dead starlight poured through my mind as ectoplasm shimmered through my veins. Bloody Mary was pulling me back there, to the future, in the near past, where I could not change a thing. I wouldn't let that happen, not with Dianne in sight.

I charged forward as the starlight shone through me. Bloody Mary's ectoplasm disintegrated as I tore at the dead memories swirling around me. Jolts of static electricity shot from my fingertips.

Dianne was nearly at the end of the drive-thru now, tumbling across the front of cars, laughing maniacally as she stole a bag of food from the cashier. Bloody Mary's ectoplasm hung over Dianne, nearly pulling her through one of the car windows to the other side. Dianne tore at the bag. She unwrapped a hamburger and devoured it so quickly I was afraid she might choke.

The ectoplasm wrapped around Dianne's neck as I focused on my neuroflash and channeled it through my veins. Bloody Mary wanted me in a state of rage. But I was growing stronger, capable of seeing through the hatred possessed in her memories.

"Show me, Bloody Mary, the other side of your mirror."

I blasted the ectoplasm through the narrow drive-thru lane, dissolving some of the dead memories hovering around Dianne's shoulders, but they were too strong. They tugged on her, slithering across her neck.

She gasped as they dragged her to the other side of the street. I charged after her, darting between cars on one of San Diego's busiest streets.

My stomach dropped as Bloody Mary's ectoplasm pulled her to the center of the intersection. But Dianne was only half aware of the terrors that hovered around her. She screamed with joy as she finished the last bite of her hamburger and waved the wrapper in the air, announcing to the world that she had just finished eating.

Bloody Mary's ectoplasm trailed to the other end of the trolley crossing and formed into the outline of the man who had haunted me before. But he looked different. When he smiled, his lips pressed deeper into his transparent skin, revealing the death that lived inside of him. He had evolved significantly, his form towering over us.

"Dianne," he said, Bloody Mary's voice speaking through him. "Do you wish to know what is waiting for you on the other side?"

She turned toward him. She started walking, hypnotized, stumbling over the railway. The trolley's bells began to chime. The crossing signs went down. Red and yellow lights flashed in the darkness.

"Dianne!" I yelled. But she couldn't hear me. She could only hear their voices, merged together through an infinite, starless void, entrancing her.

"Let her go!" I said, the ectoplasm churning through my veins.

I launched into the air, catapulting to the street lights. I reached for the metal pole and spun in an arc until I caught purchase and stood on its wobbling frame, sending the crows and pigeons flying off into the night. Even the wildlife knew they were in the presence of ghosts.

I aimed my hands at his shifting form below. I shot a burst of ectoplasm through the darkness. It pierced through his skin, half of his body melting to the floor. He screamed as Dianne laughed and laughed, dancing across the metal railway.

The railway crossing bars came down, pushing her to the floor.

The man descended into the shadows and reappeared next to her. His hands stretched outward, elongating into tendrils, trapping her there. The trolley's horn blared as she lay there, helpless.

"Dianne!"

"There's nothing you can do," Bloody Mary said. "She is going to die sooner or later, so why not now?"

"Because she still has a life to live."

Dianne was no longer laughing. Perhaps she could sense the ectoplasm pulling at her from beyond. Perhaps she could even hear Bloody Mary's voice, speaking through that infinite place, pulling her closer to death. She was entranced by the man's eyes and trapped in place, screaming a bloodcurdling cry as the trolley lights shone from about a hundred feet away.

I flew off the streetlight and rushed toward Dianne, flying through the sky, propelled by the ectoplasm that had always been in my heart. I reached for her arms, but my body only went through hers.

"That's right," Bloody Mary said. "There's nothing you can do but watch as your sister slowly dies."

"That's not true. I saved her back then, and here, now, I will save her again. Because while you are possessed by reflections, I am possessed by memories."

Shadows fell over us as the trolley burst through the end of the street, its spotlight looming over us. I placed my hands together and merged the light shooting from my fingertips into a giant orb of ectoplasm. I aimed straight at the man's scar-like smile.

"See you on the other side," I said.

I launched the energy straight into his core.

His face melted as the light tore through him, his grasp on Dianne fading. The ectoplasm shattered into infinite reflections, dissolving as the trolley's spotlight inched closer to Dianne.

She gasped and crawled to the other side of the railway, seconds away from being eviscerated by the trolley, her feet nearly caught under the wheels.

I flew there, hovering, watching Dianne as she looked through the rushing windows. Her eyes met mine, but they looked through me. "You almost killed me," I thought I heard her say, but the trolley was too loud and I could only see her lips moving through the windows.

I started crying, then, and before I knew it, Dianne ran away, again. She was released from Bloody Mary's ectoplasm but still ran into toward the darkness, unaware that I had just saved her, just as I had many times before.

My stomach dropped. It was my own fault. I had let my emotions get the best of me. I shouldn't have gotten out of my car to help her. If I hadn't tried, she never would have run off into the streets that night.

"Why are you doing this to me, Bloody Mary?" I waited for a response, but she was gone, too. She had faded away with the shadows, at least for now.

"You might be trying to trap me here, in these memories, but I'm not afraid of you. I am not helpless to these moments any more. I will show you that I can change my future. "

I floated to the trolley window, hovered in the darkness, and neuroflashed through to the other side.

CHAPTER FIFTEEN

Some spirits were never meant to come back to life.

I made a grave mistake, Erica, one that had severe consequences. I didn't mean to. I promise. It was only the natural progression of things.

When I hit rock bottom, when I was about to take my very last breath, some divine starlight had decided to shine on me, filling me with an eternal warmth, granting me a new sense of purpose in life. I was no longer afraid, because I could transcend death itself. Some cosmic voice had chosen to speak to me, endowing me with this eternal power that was waiting for me here, in the void. It was my destiny, and it had truly given me a new sense of direction. I had become so lost after the death of my parents, and, finally, I had a reason to keep going.

I became something like a guardian angel, floating eternally through the Oregon Trail, watching over those who had fallen. And just when those poor spirits thought their time had finally come, I brought them back to life by channeling the power of the infinite starlight sparkling through my fingertips.

I gained an incredible amount of perspective. The ectoplasm wasn't just a reflection of the infinite starlight above. It also contained the memories of the universe, the memories of the living, the memories of the dead, circulating between two realms, between two stars that shone light-years apart.

Things became much clearer then, in the looking glass. My reflection was changing. I was no longer the girl I used to be, and I was becoming something else entirely. I did not know if I was mortal, or immortal, or temporarily undead, but I was most likely something in between. I was a ghost, in limbo, suspended in time as the stars shared their secrets with me. By saving others from the coldness of the trail, perhaps I would also save myself.

You learn a lot of things when you become a vessel of light. When the ectoplasm churns through your veins, you see things differently. I learned that when people are on the brink of life and death, and they claim to see a light at the end of the tunnel, it's because they actually do. There has always been someone—or something—like me, pulling those spirits back to their bodies as they are drawn into the deepest, darkest parts of the universe by the gravity of their memories. You cannot weigh memories in ounces, but you can measure them throughout time, how memories are linked together infinitely.

I soon discovered that the stars were always there for us, just as Father had told me. But stars only know the quality of their light if they are connected in a constellation. If I wanted to bring someone back to life, all I had to do was help their lost souls remember the warmth of that starlight, the meaning of their existence to their family and friends. Even in moments of their deepest suffering, I could show them this light that waited for them at the end of the tunnel. The memories contained there were the memories that would never be, if their hearts stopped beating. They needed to press on, to survive, to make it back to the other side.

Their memories were still being created. If those humans died, the stars themselves might be in danger. Memories were a lot like the stars, I realized. If one were to stop shining, the rest might only see darkness and forget their own light. If I did not continue resurrecting the families that were never meant to die, that were supposed to make it to the other side of the trail, then the entire sky might be in danger of falling. Life as we knew it would fold into itself, crumbling under the weight of absent memories, of starlight that would never reach their true potential.

How wrong it turned out I was.

At the time, I thought I was doing the right thing. It all made sense to me. My locket granted me an infinite source of strength when I was surrounded by an infinite void of darkness. It simply made sense for me to transfer this divine source of energy to those who had perished on their journey, just like my parents.

I had become a conduit for the universe, keeping its memories alive as they surged through me. But soon enough, one thing became very apparent to me.

I had been deceived.

I wasn't just channeling the starlight. Somewhere along the way, my locket had reflected something else, something even more sinister that had died long ago.

One night, as I recharged my power through the looking glass, I had unknowingly reflected those stars that were never there to begin with, at least not in my lifetime, anyways. But I still saw them in the mirror, like they were here, right above me. They were distant memories of what they used to be. Something about the ectoplasm was different that night. I could feel it in my bones. And when I placed my hand on the locket, preparing myself to revive the fallen souls I had stumbled upon, it felt as though I was now suspended in an infinite void between the memories of those stars, because what I didn't know was, the stars were already dead.

They had died long, long ago.

It became clear to me that Mary's voice had spoken to me from there, from that infinite realm of death where memories go to die. She had made me believe she was something like Saint Mary herself, but she was much different. And she was far from benevolent. Her distorted reflection had been created in that place where memories have already died. A place where there is nothing but wickedness.

I was playing a deadly game of dice with Death. Somewhere in space, the stars that shine onto us are already dead, and when I channeled the dead starlight, I opened up doors that were sealed long ago.

They had been waiting for me.

Those men who had murdered my parents must've known that one day, I would become so lost in my new reflection that I wouldn't think twice about raising the dead who were meant to remain dead. Sometimes in life, you cannot blame yourself for the decisions you made. But when you are staring in the face of true evil, and you have somehow helped that evil come back to life, there is no one else to blame but the person staring back at you in the mirror.

I know why Father gave me that locket. He wanted somebody to protect it, to understand the depth of power it contained. But I was young. I was naive. I should have learned more about the stars before falling into them. I should have known it was a trap from the start.

I remember that night like it was yesterday, and it could have been, here, in the Interstate. Strange, how memory works. That night, as I pulled up to an encampment, the silence was so deafening that I could hear my own heart beating. I became hyperaware, hearing my own footsteps as though they came from someone else. I was already drifting away from my mortal body, though I wasn't able to comprehend it like that at the time. Because the ectoplasm knew something I didn't.

It was afraid.

That dead starlight was there, trapped in the bodies waiting for me to bring them back from the dead, half-buried in the snow. Those men—those memories—that had slaughtered my parents were waiting for me in the shadows.

I hopped off Bessie, tethered her to the nearest wagon, and approached the bodies sprawled across the ground. At first glance, the entire scene appeared to be yet another one of those terrible bloodbaths that I had encountered, a tragic toll of traveling along the trail. I focused on the stars as ectoplasm surged through me, but it was a different sensation, like a coldness burning through my body. I thought this was because I had grown stronger, and I had merely adapted to this electrical charge that swam through my system. I could raise anything from the dead at that point.

I took a deep breath. I waved my hands over the bodies, light dripping from my fingers like honey onto their skin, melting the snow.

But in the darkness, I saw that smile. A smile like a scar.

It was the very man who had killed my parents.

But it wasn't him anymore.

He was never human to begin with. As the ectoplasm filled his body, he lifted himself up, propelled by the shadows of dead memories.

A coldness filled his eyes, like dead starlight reincarnated. I backed up into the empty wagon as he became aware of his reawakening. He brushed off his shoulders, took a deep breath, and sighed.

"Well, well, well, what do we have here…" He looked around the camp as his fellow outlaws stirred back to life. "Looks like our plan done worked well, now, didn't it?"

The ectoplasm around my body had diminished entirely. I was cold again, so cold for the first time in months that I started shivering. The amount of pain and hunger that I had avoided fell back onto me like an avalanche. An instant agony overwhelmed me, and I could do nothing but sit there and watch as the ectoplasm now sparked from his fingertips.

I had given that dead starlight its power back.

They had already been exiled to Hell, and I had brought them back to life.

That night, I lost control of everything around me. As I said before, Erica, some monsters are born, and some monsters are created. In that moment, I had created the very monster that would soon destroy everything I knew in sight.

He started shifting, then. Something deep within his soul was finally resurfacing. Something within his body stirred awake, his skin crawling with invisible bugs that burrowed through his arms, his chest, every organ, his skin breaking out in goosepimples that transformed into shadow mounds that ate him from within.

The dead starlight was eating him alive.

As the shadows diminished, the moonlight revealed a figure cloaked in shadowy ectoplasm. It shimmered crimson in the moonlight. It turned to me and smiled, scar-like.

"You have pulled me through the looking glass, and now, I will show you the other side."

I knew who it was, then—*what* it was, rather. I had brought back Bloody Mary's reflection from that place in space.

I shivered as she ripped the locket from my neck, placed my hand against the looking glass, and sent me through to the other side in her place.

CHAPTER SIXTEEN

DIANNE

Hey Erica,

Hope you're doin' well. Tour's been fun. Just ended today, technically last night when we had our last show. My ankle's feeling better. But I'm still taking the meds 'cuz it's makin' everything easier. I'll probably stop soon. It's just an interim. What does that word even mean? It's helping me survive the in-between. It's just temporary. It's not a real high, anyways, just a small smoothing sensation. Hopefully, I'll get to fill you in sooner or later.

I know this sounds kinda strange, but today, when the airplane took off, I felt like I was going somewhere else. Not headed back home. Felt like I was flying into the sky, where I'd be, always. Maybe it was because I was already high. Everything was blurring together. The tour. Your Facebook profile and the Throwback Thursdays I saw. I stared out the airplane window, hoping that by focusing on the horizon, there might be a chance I would sober up. But it felt endless, like I had never really left the ground at all.

Below, the plains stretched into the distance, intersecting with mountains that were covered in different shades of green, almost like an emerald quilt or something. It was almost peaceful, like this place on the horizon was a destination of its own. I wondered what it would be like to live in times where there was no city life, no concert halls, no tours.

We hit a brief moment of turbulence. Or maybe I was just getting a little more high. The seatbelt lights flashed on. Fran laughed and fastened her seatbelt.

"You afraid?" she asked.

"What?"

"Got a fear of flying? Or did you bite off a little more than you could chew?"

"Maybe both."

"You high right now?"

"*Fran.*"

"What?"

"Can you please not?"

She leaned in. "Nobody can hear. For all they know, we could be talking about anything. And I'm sure there are plenty of people onboard who are hiding something, too."

She was right. The way I'm typing this to you is like fiction, isn't it? *Lol.* I looked over my shoulder, and everybody seemed to be living in their own world. First class had a way of doing that to people, and even though I belonged anywhere *but* the first class, I pretended like I fit in perfectly, silencing my rumbling stomach with another sip of white wine.

"You sure you're okay to drink that, Dianne?"

"You're telling me? Very funny."

"Well, if it's not already common sense by now, I meant to tell you earlier that it's probably not the best idea to take a bunch of drugs before you're 20,000 feet up in the air. The pressure up here can do weird stuff to people. One time I had a migraine so bad I thought my brain was gonna explode."

"And what about you? Where are you at today?"

"I have a high enough tolerance. I'm buzzing, but just a little. How's your ankle, by the way? Seems like you can walk on it just fine now."

"Well. It's definitely…better."

"So, you don't need my help anymore?"

"Well…hmmm…" I looked out the window again. The mountains seemed smaller, distant. We were higher up now. Everything seemed far away. In a few hours, everything would go back to normal. We would land. I would go back home. I would be alone in my apartment, preparing myself for the next tour, until we did it all over again. But what really waited for me there, back home?

Not you. I wish you were waiting for me. Remember when we were kids and I made you wish upon a shooting star at your prom, when it probably wasn't even there? Where do you think those wishes go, when there is nothing at the other end hearing us?

"Because, I mean, if you want some more when we get back," whispered Fran, "we can find a way to arrange that."

"I don't know."

"Yes, you do."

The airplane rocked slightly. My stomach did an aerial flip.

"I don't feel too hot right now."

"Knew it." Francesca sighed, reached into her purse, and pulled out another bag of pills. "Need something to balance it out?"

"How did you get that here?" I sat up in my chair and looked over my shoulder again. "Wow."

"Play it cool."

"This isn't cool."

"Who are you worried about? I'm just a friend giving a friend a gift. If you act guilty, somebody will actually think you are."

I took the bag and slipped it into the front pocket of my jacket.

"What are these?"

"The opposite of the ones you took. It's like ibuprofen, but a lot stronger. That way you won't have to take a lot. They'll counter-balance the effect."

"How'd you get it through TSA?"

She laughed. "I'm a pro by now, duh. And what'd you do? Take them all before you walked through the body scanner?"

"Well, it was either that or get caught."

She raised an eyebrow. "You took *all* of them?" I nodded. "Well, then, what're you waiting for?"

Something dropped to the bottom of my stomach, and my body felt off, like a part of me was about to topple over, each organ ready to purge whatever was left inside. I thought I knew my tolerance, but I don't think I did. It's crazy how much your life can change within two months. Especially when you're on drugs. Ha.

I walked to the bathroom. There was a short line. Kids. Parents. They were all completely unaware that I was fading. Or cross-faded. What was I doing, taking these things in front of people, in front of potential fans? I hope you don't think any less of me, Erica. I never meant to fall so hard into this stuff.

When it was my turn, I slammed the bathroom door behind me as quickly as I could. I braced myself on the countertop. I took five deep breaths, then ten. Acid swirled at the bottom of my throat, but instead of fighting the sensation, I made peace with it. I swallowed. I didn't want to get sick again.

I looked up, and there you were, in the bathroom mirror.

You were floating right there, Erica. Watching me through the mirror, hovering over the sink, staring right through me.

I gasped and backed into the toilet. A strange surge of adrenaline ran through me, like a happy anger. I banged my ankle into the wall.

Why were you following me, Erica, when you didn't even want to speak to me?

Why were you haunting me, like a ghost?

I stood there, staring at the mirror, crying, thinking of all the memories we had already missed out on, all the memories that never would be, if we didn't fix this sometime soon. I felt so far away from you, even though you were right there, transparent, starlight shining through your skin. But you and I knew the bad blood would never go away, until we did something about it. We were distanced. We were literally in the same room today, sort of, and still, you couldn't even acknowledge me.

And then you disappeared, as though you were never there in the first place.

I'm not gonna lie. You scared the living hell out of me. I didn't want you to see me like this.

Did you see me today, Erica, like this?

I cupped water into my hands, splashed my face, and downed the pills as quickly as I could. I felt the medicine trailing down my throat, inch by inch. I took a few deep breaths as it settled into place. The feeling was instantaneous, counteracting everything else.

The pills made the ghost in the mirror go away.

It was just me, high, up in the sky.

Someone knocked on the door.

"Dianne?" Francesca's voice seemed miles away. "You okay?"

I nodded. I was fine.

Just fine.

-Dianne

CHAPTER SEVENTEEN

I neuroflashed back to the past, my mind searing with memories, a sweet pool of sensations and sights and sounds flowing through my brain like a burst of warm spring air. I was nowhere and everywhere, floating through the void, and then my body froze as the world melted into itself.

~ ~ ~

I thawed and materialized into the memory beyond, tumbling through a playground's plastic window onto a swing set, where I sat with Dianne.

"So, yeah, Erica…I've noticed something recently."

The ectoplasm faded around my skin as I swung back and forth on our neighborhood park's plastic swing set. We were at the end of the cul-de-sac, and our family's house was on the opposite end of the street. Some of our neighbors liked to call it the Candyland house, because from this perspective, its light maroon and vanilla chimney twisted into the sky like the swirly tip of a fresh batch of cotton candy. It struck me as entirely funny how my perception of distance was vastly different during childhood. Here, we could have been on the other side of the world, at the other end of the Oregon Trail, leagues away from home.

It was just the two of us, now.

Dianne was swinging next to me, rocking like a pendulum, swaying to a steady beat until she kicked her feet in a wild burst that was so powerful, she almost reached the top of the swing set. But she always stopped before she circled back around. That's how she was, always underestimating her own strength.

"What's wrong?" I stopped swinging, letting my feet drag across the sand until I reached a full stop. "Did I do something?"

Dianne laughed. She recently had just gotten her braces off during spring break, and she didn't realize how much of a difference that had made in her mood. She was always laughing, but not in a condescending way. She possessed some new inner joy, like she was seeing the world through rose-colored glasses, and it was rubbing off on me, even though not long ago, I had experienced one of the worst days of my life.

I had seen a monster in the mirror.

And I couldn't tell anyone.

Because nobody would believe me.

Not even my own sister.

"No, not at all," said Dianne. "I just wanted to check in with you about something."

I didn't realize it back then, but in my body, now, in living retrospect, I could identify the feeling as a trigger of anxiety. My hands grew clammy against the metal chains holding up the swing, and my breathing became short. I wouldn't know what anxiety attacks were like until I was in high school, but I shouldn't have hid my feelings from my sister. I could tell her anything, except about what I had seen floating through the mirror.

"I'm fine."

"Hey…" She stopped swinging. "You know you can talk to me about anything, right?"

"I know."

"I heard Mom and Dad talking the other night."

"Oh."

"Do you wanna know what they said?"

"I mean, hmmm…was it about me?"

She nodded. "They're worried about you. And I don't mean to tell you that to, like, make you scared or anything. That's actually the opposite of what I'm trying to do. Not my, uh, what's it called again?"

"Your tension."

"*In*tention. I knew that. *Lol.* Right."

"Yeah. Right."

She smiled again, flashing her brand-new pearly straight teeth. But I didn't feel like smiling anymore. My stomach filled with something like dread. We were having our first heart-to-heart, our first "real" adult conversation, even though I was eight and she was ten and we had no idea how to push past the barriers we had built around our hearts.

"I've noticed that you've been acting a little—"

"A little what? Cranky? Bratty? That other 'B' word?" I asked.

"Jeez, take it easy. No. Gosh. What would the right word be?"

She looked off into the distance, staring at our house, searching somewhere in the sky for answers. In the distance, Dad's car pulled up. That meant it was around five, right when he came home back from work. I didn't know it back then, but in this moment, now, I could tell Dianne was trying to be careful with me, because she knew I had become delicate. She was actually being more sensitive than I had ever given her credit for.

"Ahh. I got the word. I think the word is…quiet. Quieter. That's not a real word, though. More quiet. Ever since winter break, you don't wanna watch scary movies anymore, and you haven't wanted to watch me play video games. I know there's another word for this. Maybe…withdrawn?"

I nodded in a silent agreement—or maybe in embarrassment. It's amazing, what retrospect could do. It made me not only miss those moments, but it also helped me see things differently, revealing hidden parts of myself and others around me that I never knew existed. She knew what I was going through, though. Dianne always had my back, even if I never admitted it at the time. She was my sister, a true reflection of myself. I wouldn't have become the adult I was now if not for her.

"I'm sorry," I said. "I don't mean to be."

"You don't have to apologize. And you don't have to be quiet around me. Even if you gotta talk about the harder stuff, the more difficult stuff, you know, you can always talk to me."

My heart leapt. In that moment, I wanted to spill everything I had seen in the mirror. I wished I could also tell her about the things I couldn't tell her, about how I had seen those posts on my timeline, just last night, about how she had died, about how she would win a national singing show, about how she would be cold one night, while walking endlessly through the streets of San Diego. Although my brain possessed this knowledge, my former self didn't have the words to express this, and suddenly, I forgot to mention this to her.

"There is something, actually."

"Here. Let's go sit somewhere where we can talk easier. You know, without distractions."

She grabbed my hand and led me to the park bench. We walked through the deserted desert of the playground, our shoeprints creating silly, swirly shapes in the sand. The bench was literally only five feet away, which seemed kind of funny, even at the time, but we both knew it was something adults did. They always had a moment where they shifted, where they went somewhere else. They needed to sit across from each other or side by side to have a heart-to-heart.

We were just reflecting what our parents did. Not like mockingbirds, but new birds, trying to spread our wings and help each other lift into the sky. She was always there, the wind beneath my wings, helping me soar to new heights. I felt like crying, then. It had happened in that moment but it also happened in this moment, when I knew that I would truly be on my own, in the future.

"I am proud of you for wanting to talk." She said this with a feigned gentle authority, a certain kind of assertiveness, almost like when Mom or Dad applauded us for doing the right thing by telling on each other when we did something bad, which rarely happened. We weren't normally tattletales, but sometimes we had tales to tattle. "I am here to listen."

The way she said *I am* instead of *I'm* struck me as mind-blowing. She had never talked so directly. That's when it finally sunk in. We were having a real conversation. If I didn't at least tell her what was on my mind, then it would be my own fault. I would be building my own wall around my heart.

"Thanks. Maybe I do need to talk. I didn't mean to not talk. It's just that…lately, I've been feeling a little scared."

"Scared?" The concern on her face, or acknowledgement, or a concerned acknowledgement, made me a little more scared to talk.

"Yeah. It's hard to explain. Not scared like in a jumpy kind of way, like when someone scares you in a haunted house and you want to scream 'cuz the monster just popped out at you in the movie. Scared because of things that can happen in life."

"Like what kind of things?"

"You know. Everything. Well, not *everything*, but a lot of things." She remained silent, and I added, "Like the future. Stuff like that."

"So, you are afraid of the future. That's okay, Erica. It is normal to feel that way. I mean, we've got a whole lot of future ahead of us, don't we?"

"Yeah…"

"I think when every kid graduates from third grade to fourth, and then from sixth to seventh, and then eighth to ninth, and then from twelfth to college, and then from adulthood to old people land, there's always a moment where you tell yourself, wow, I'm old."

"Do you think that's how it is?"

"Yeah, probably. I mean, I am in the sixth grade, after all. I've been through a lot."

"I just can't believe I'm nine already. And then I'm actually going to be ten in a few months. *Ten*."

"Yeah. You're gonna be an old hag, like me!" She pulled her hood over her head and pretended to be an old witch, the wicked witch of the North, floating on a broomstick, searching through miles of fantastical forests. She lifted her hands as though she were casting a deadly spell. "You better watch out. I'm gonna get ya!"

It made me laugh, then, and I remembered the warmth that she could provide to me in an instant. We were so tuned into each other that when she shifted frequencies, I couldn't help but giggle, even though deep down, I was afraid.

I didn't want to tell her what had frightened me so much.

She must have sensed this because she pulled her hood down and looked concerned again. "Okay. Sorry. Big sister moment. I had to."

"You're so silly. What's it like, on the other side? You know, being older?"

"It's fun. You get to be more tall. You can go on rollercoasters that you couldn't go on before. You get to buy cool new binders for different subjects. Dad always says that once you turn eighteen, you can buy lotto tickets, but I'm not so sure I wanna do that because I'd probably waste a lot of money, just like with Pokemon cards."

"Yeah. Me too, actually."

"But it's really not so scary, the future. You just grow another year older, but that also means you get another candle on a cake, which helps make your wish come true even more."

"Is that how it works?"

"Sure. Why not?"

"But what happens after that, when you grow so old that you then go to sleep and then you die?"

She opened her mouth to speak but hesitated. She nodded, realizing the weight of my thoughts.

"That's a good question. Did something make you think about that?"

"Yeah."

"Yeah? I think I might know what."

"You do?"

"Come on, *Er-Bear*. I'm your sister. We're like, practically the same person. And when you're happy, I'm happy. I know everything about you."

"If you know what's scaring me, then why are you asking?"

"Was it when we were playing Bloody Mary?" My eyes widened. I frantically looked around, seeing if anyone else could hear. Dianne added, "Don't worry, I won't say her name again. And, besides, she can't come here unless there's a mirror."

"No. Please. You don't understand…"

"So, was that what it was?" she asked. I nodded. "Really?"

I buried my face in my hands. I didn't want to give that monster a chance of seeing me from the other side of the mirror.

"Oh, no. Erica, I don't mean that in a bad way. I'm not saying it like you shouldn't have been scared. I'm just glad that's all it was. I don't mean to make it sound like I'm making your pain about that situation any less. Diminishing your pain? Is that what the word is?"

We sat there for a moment. I heard Mom and Dad talking on the porch at the other end of the cul-de-sac. That night, they were making one of our favorite meals, mac and cheese. But it all felt so far away. Nobody, not even me, really understood how to express these weird emotions about death.

"Well, I want to let you know that I didn't see anything. In the mirror. But that doesn't mean that *you* didn't. Sometimes two people can be in the same situation and be on two sides of the coin, even when they are on the same side of the mirror, like we were."

"That's exactly right."

"What did you see, then?"

I bit my lip. "It's hard to explain. A lot of things. It might take a while. I know you're hungry, too. I can smell the mac and cheese from here."

"It can wait." She smiled again. "I have time."

"Okay…" I shifted in my seat, and for once, probably for the first time in my life, I felt like I was having a real adult conversation, too. I didn't know it then, but sometimes you crossed certain thresholds in your life without realizing it, and you didn't need to wait for an extra candle on your cake. "When we said her name, the third time, I saw something."

"You did? What did it look like?"

"It wasn't what you'd think. It was worse, actually. I don't think she is evil, but trapped, maybe. Like all ghosts. But obviously, some ghosts are bad. Everyone knows that. But some are just stuck there, waiting to get out."

"So, you saw her, then?"

"Yes, and no. It was really weird. I was everywhere and nowhere. It was like I was living in two moments, or two dreams, that were happening at the same time."

"Wow."

"Yeah. You know when people say they saw their life flash before their eyes?"

"Yeah?"

"Yeah. It was like that."

"So, you didn't see her."

"I did see her."

"But you don't know what she looked like."

"I do. But it all depends on who is looking, I think. For me, she was a shadow at first, and that shadow turned into a light, and then in the mirror I saw hands reaching out, and then it was a flash of everything, a light so bright I couldn't see for a sec."

"Hey. It's okay—"

The words kept tumbling out of me: "And then everything melted like snow and there were shadows everywhere, shadow hands and shadow arms and the planets were falling out of the sky and then I saw you, and I saw me, but we were older, a lot older, like *old* old, twenty or something, and then it was us, but not us, and then the shadows were there again, and they kept pulling us down, and they showed our reflections and we were different, much different, like two different people…"

"Hey. It's okay, Erica. Take a deep breath."

Somewhere, in my peripheral view, I could sense Bloody Mary hovering around me. She did not want me to share my story, but I wouldn't let her stop me. In order to keep her at bay, I needed to press on.

"And then it flashed again, my mind," I said, "and then I saw everything and then you weren't there, Dianne. *You weren't there anymore.* You were gone and then the darkness was everywhere, but then I saw you here, now, and then the light came back and then we were back here, talking about it, like we were already here, like this moment already happened."

"All from that one moment?"

"Yeah."

"Like déjà vu."

"No."

"Dang." I could hear in Dianne's voice that she was growing afraid, too. Maybe in that moment, we were both not ready to be adults, to pretend that we knew the answers to such difficult things. "Yeah. That does sound terrifying. I'm sorry you had that moment, Erica. I had something like that once, in my dreams, where that type of stuff happened, where the sky fell and I was falling. Again, it's a normal thing, to be really afraid of something you don't know. Like the future."

"Sometimes I don't want the future to happen, Dianne. I mean, the far future. I want the near future, like tomorrow, but sometimes I don't want to grow up."

"Well, you got a lotta cool years ahead of you, my dude."

"Do you think you can really get to know someone, by sharing just a few memories, a few moments, with them?"

"As long as they're real ones, sure. I'm lucky to have many moments with you. But let's just think of tomorrow, then, yeah? And then tomorrow's tomorrow after that. And then we'll go from there."

Dianne hugged me. At the end of the cul-de-sac, I heard Dad's voice, telling us that dinner was ready.

"What do you think is on the other side, Dianne?"

"The other side of what? The mirror, or like, life?"

"Both, maybe."

She shrugged. "Like Dad says, maybe we'll find out when we're older. But for right now, Erica, you don't have to worry about any of that. You had a moment, and now it's gone. It's in the past. You have nothing to be afraid of, because I'm here with you, now. And if you're ever afraid, if you think you see her shadow again…Mary's…then just tell me and I'll make it go away." She smiled again. "That's what sisters are for, right? Besides, when you look at yourself in the mirror, remember that we're practically the same person. We share the same blood, after all."

"Thanks," I said, shivers shooting down my spine. "Thanks for listening."

"You're welcome," Dianne said. But it wasn't Dianne any longer.

It was Bloody Mary, speaking through her from lightyears away.

Adrenaline surged through my veins as I tried to manifest the ectoplasm in my blood, preparing to attack her at a moment's notice. But I couldn't feel the gravity of the stars shining within me, because this memory wasn't strong enough yet. I hadn't given Dianne my goodbye hug, the one that would empower me and supply me with courage for the rest of the day.

So I turned around, ready to face Bloody Mary, here, in my childhood neighborhood, in order to hug Dianne again as we lived another moment just a heartbeat away from home. She was nowhere in sight.

"Do you see me now, Erica?" I turned around and there she was, hovering in Dianne's eyes. She had become a distant star, hidden in an undiscovered galaxy, twinkling dimly as she spoke. "Are the shadows gone? What do I look like to you?"

"Get out. Get out of my sister's head."

"And why would I want to do that? Don't you remember? You were both here, talking about how you were right *there* at your house, when you had called my name. Are you saying you did not really wish to see me? Are you lying to me, Erica?"

"No. It's just—"

"It's just what? You were afraid to see me?" In Dianne's eyes, Bloody Mary grew brighter until she shone with such intensity that I had to cover my face. "Tell the truth, you scaredy-cat. Are you afraid of me?"

I opened my eyes, hoping to catch sight of Bloody Mary's true form. A flash of energy pulsed from Dianne's eyes as ectoplasm burst through her fingertips.

I ducked underneath the park bench as tendrils of light slithered across the sidewalk to our house at the end of the cul-de-sac.

"No!" I screamed, helpless to the dead memories swirling around me. "Mom! Dad!"

The ectoplasm tore through the wooden fences and squeaky gates and rusted lawn chairs, through broken Razer scooters and shredded basketball hoops and frayed jump ropes, through all of the simple, happy things we had held onto as children that now only existed within our minds. The light pierced through the world that had defined me and left a dark void in its wake.

I crawled from underneath the park bench and ran after. Starlight shifted in my veins. We were hovering there, now, back then, forever, in that place between the dead stars.

"Do you wish to stay here, Erica, where you can be blissfully unaware of Dianne's fate? Do you wish to stay here, where you will be safe from your future?"

"I have many more moments to share with Dianne from this point. I wouldn't know who I am if I couldn't experience those. I wouldn't let anything take that away."

"So be it. If that is what you wish, then I will trap their spirits here, instead."

At the other end of the cul-de-sac, ectoplasm crawled under my house's front gate, wrapped around the walls, and crept across the roof. Somewhere inside, Mom and Dad were sitting, talking about their days, unaware of Bloody Mary's presence.

I was only halfway across the street when I felt the power of the stars shoot through my blood. I launched a pulse of light at the roof. Bloody Mary's dead starlight shimmered and merged with mine.

"I will never let you go back through that mirror. Not when my sister is still alive."

Dianne was standing across the street from me now. She turned to me and frowned.

"Strange. I can feel your memories but now, it is more difficult for me to see through to the other side of my mirror." I could hear Dianne's voice coming back into Bloody Mary's. Dianne was regaining her senses, even though Bloody Mary's reflection twinkled in her eyes. "Your life flashed before your eyes and now you are growing stronger, Erica. It appears our memories are blurring together. But that does not phase me. I know what you are most afraid of, and I will send you there, to those memories."

The ectoplasm flashed across the horizon. A booming thunder echoed throughout the neighborhood. Houses wobbled in place as their walls began melting into the infinite shadows underneath.

The dead memories rained upon me as I sank into the ground to the universe below, searching for Bloody Mary.

I ran in place, frozen by the terrors I saw there, of the futures we would not see if I did not succeed, until I created so much friction that I shot ectoplasm into Bloody Mary's memories, and I crystallized into the weight of their gravity, somewhere between the stars, and I neuroflashed further through the Interstate.

CHAPTER EIGHTEEN

DIANNE

Hi, Erica,

Got bad news. Fainted today at the airport. Probably should go to the doctor but don't really want to. Gonna let my bloodstream settle down, if you know what I mean.

It was pretty scary. When we arrived at baggage claim, I got sad because I thought of you again. It hit me like a freight train. That's a horrible expression, *btw*. I realized just how little I had left to come home to. The drugs made the flight speed by, and for a moment, things felt timeless. Later, though, everything hit me hard, and I came crashing down.

Everyone else had someone waiting for them by the airport exit. I pretended to smile, maybe for the fans. I must have been the only person on tour to not have someone back home waiting for me to return. I had no welcoming party, no hugs or happy tears, no significant other to embrace. I know I won't hear from you, Erica, at least not until things cool down, whenever that happens. I'm trying my best here.

But something else filled the loneliness. It was that feeling of warmth spreading through my chest. I think the pills really started working then. I mean, they were working before, but now, it was different. It made it easier to not see you there, to not hear your laughter again. I miss you. A lot.

I was about to pick up my bag from luggage claim when fans came stampeding out of nowhere, snapping photos on their phones, pushing slips of paper and receipts in front of us for autographs.

"Dianne!"

"Over here."

"Sign this!"

The world melted in the flash of lights. I remembered being in this moment before, but that couldn't have been the case, because I had never been to this terminal. My memory was blurring together. Maybe it was the drugs. Hopefully not.

I pressed my sunglasses against my nose. Didn't want anyone to see my bloodshot eyes, to be completely honest. I was high, much higher than I'd ever been before, very much so. I had gotten off the plane but, boy oh boy, was I soaring across the skies now. It was fun, and the attention made it all the more wonderful. Even standing in a sea of people, of frantic fans who didn't really know me, at least I had someone saying my name. I would enjoy the spotlight while it lasted.

Because, after all, I had struck gold. I was famous now.

This will be the new normal, at least for the time being. The pills made me think of you less, not because I didn't think of you, obviously, but because I usually think of you so often that it tears me apart.

As the fans retreated, I picked up my bag and blacked out.

-Dianne

CHAPTER NINETEEN

That very day, Erica, when Bloody Mary trapped me in the locket, I neuroflashed back to the same day my parents were murdered.

I jerked awake as though out of a dream, maybe even a nightmare. In that moment, I couldn't tell the difference. I found myself lying in the wagon, a new locket hanging around my neck. How could there be two mirrors, when Bloody Mary had the other?

It didn't matter, though. In that moment, I was overjoyed. I had gotten what I had wished for. I was finally able to see my parents again, and that was worth whatever pain I had endured to get back here. Still, I needed to remain calm, so I would not reveal myself. If I played my cards right, maybe I even had a chance to change our destiny.

I opened the locket and placed my hand against the looking glass, hoping to regain the ectoplasm, but nothing shone. For some reason, this memory was slightly different, the timing of things moved around a fraction of a few minutes, but that didn't necessarily mean that the ending of it would change.

That meant only one thing.

Bloody Mary's reflections were waiting in the darkness ahead, and it was all part of her plan. For some reason, she knew that the longer she waited to reveal herself, the more terrified I would become. This time, though, I was gifted with the ability of hindsight. I knew what was waiting for me, and when you know the monster is approaching, at least you have a chance to fight back.

I quickly thought of my most recent memories, of how I raised those poor souls from the dead, of how I had seen Bloody Mary possess the man who would kill my parents. I tried to remember what it was like to have the ectoplasm churning through my veins in case I needed it, but right now, I could not bring this power back to me. It was left there, in the future.

I slowly but surely realized I was about to relive the worst day of my life. I couldn't let that happen. I couldn't be stuck in this forever. I needed to hold on to hope, just a little longer.

I turned the locket toward the sky. If the ectoplasm came from the stars, then I figured they must know something I didn't to guide me through this moment. Perhaps I was a star, too, shooting through the galaxies. I watched the stars reflect through the glass, tracing the constellations with my eyes, searching for clues in the skies above. Still, I saw nothing. No stars reflected their light into the mirror. A wave of cold, of fear, washed over me.

In the front of the wagon, Father hummed a gentle tune under his breath as Bessie quietly neighed in harmony. It was a folk song, something about a lone wanderer, and this time it struck me as something to take note of. Did he know that I would be flashing back to this very moment, having traveled alone for so long?

But he couldn't have possibly known what I was going through, could he? If the answer was in the locket, within the mirror, then maybe he was trying to clue me in on something. I kept these questions to myself so as to not appear delusional. Mother was already sick in her scarlet fever, lying next to me. Though the stars were shining above, they soon faded behind a thick covering of cumulus clouds, just as they had before, as though the sky itself knew what was about to happen.

I was losing sight of the stars, but I hoped they were not losing sight of me.

Something struck the wheel, and the wagon jerked viciously to the left. Bessie reared out of control, our wagon swaying in the wake of her tide. Dad stopped singing that folk song and cursed under his breath. Mom jolted from her sleep, looking around, half delirious in her sickness. I had been here before.

"Are you all right?"

"Yes." I nodded, though my eyes started to well up. I hugged Mom as tightly as I could without overwhelming her. If I would never flash back to this memory again, then I would cherish it while I still could. "Something struck the wheel."

"Macy, do you mind? Bring the lantern, if you could."

Shivers ran through my spine. Something was waiting for us there, in that place beyond the shadows. I could not reveal myself too soon. Perhaps this was the moment when I could even save them, if I acted cautiously.

I hopped off the wagon, scanning through the darkness to see where and when Marty would strike. But it was quiet, and at least for the moment, those lifeless souls were kept at bay.

"Dang wheels have been acting up for a while now, haven't they?" Dad rubbed the dirt off his hands and hopped out of the front seat. He saw the locket and smirked. "Hey…hey now, you little stinker. What've you been up to back there? Snooping through my stuff? That was supposed to be a surprise!"

I ran to Dad and gave him the biggest hug I could. I didn't want to let go. Though I had lived this memory once before, I didn't want to know what happened next.

"This locket… Father, what is in it?"

He smiled. "Well, now, it's that picture we took right before we left."

"No, Dad. What's *really* in this?"

He opened his mouth to speak but hesitated. Something shifted in his eyes, a certain kind of understanding, a knowing, like a curtain being lifted.

"Macy, we have been here before, is that so?" I nodded. "Then there is something you should know. There is a light that shines within your eyes, within your soul, one that can see through to the memories on the other-"

Before Dad could finish his sentence, two shots rang through the valley.

"Father!" I screamed as a gang of bandits surrounded us.

When I turned around, I discovered that they had all transformed into Bloody Mary's distorted reflections.

It was all my fault, I realized. In the past, which was now the future, I had summoned her from that place deep within space, where the dead starlight shines. I had made the mistake of looking into it, believing it was shining onto me.

Now, I paid the price. Her eyes were lifeless, a cloud of shadows swirling within.

"No, stay back. Father, I can't lose you again!"

But Bloody Mary's reflections surrounded our wagon and pulled Mom from the back of the wagon. In that semi-darkness, Marty's smile—Bloody Mary's smile—spread across her face, a scar revealing the hollowness within. Two gunshots rang through the night. Her reflections had just killed my parents, but this time, I wouldn't run away.

I would find a way to bring them back to life.

"Hello, Macy. We meet again."

"How dare you."

She walked forward, not walking but gliding across the earth, a shadow of illuminating ectoplasm trailing behind her. My old locket hung from her neck. I looked down at my own necklace. It sent shivers down my spine. Somehow, we had created a living duplicate of the same object.

She nodded. "That's right, Macy. Now, we both have access to the same mirror. You have your end, and I have mine. Now, if you play nice, I might just do to your parents what you did to us."

She held her hand over my parents' lifeless bodies, teasing me, tempting me.

"Please, just do it. Bring them back to life."

"Name one good reason."

"Because I love them. Just tell me what you want. Please. I'll do anything."

She lifted her arm in the air, inches away from their bodies.

"Listen, Macy. I know what it is like to die a million times over. I know what it is like to have your life ripped out from under you. But this, we cannot change this. As long as we both walk the earth, you must keep coming back to this moment."

Behind her, the other men nodded in perfect synchronization. It was then that I realized Bloody Mary was controlling them, too. That infinite place within the looking glass consumed them all.

Bloody Mary had possessed them.

I had allowed this.

I had created this monster before my very eyes.

The blood she spilled would be on my hands.

"What do you want from me?" I asked, preparing to trap her in my mirror. But even as I contemplated the ways in which I would lock her there, it seemed absurd. She was infinitely stronger than I, and I couldn't do this on my own. Not without your help, Erica.

"You toyed with destiny, Macy. You have brought back the dead. That blood was meant to shower the earth. Therefore, you must pay for that blood…with your own."

She started toward me, but then I thought of you, Erica, and you were with me, on the other side, just as you are now.

And somehow, instead of dying, I transcended through the looking glass and waited there as Bloody Mary tore through our timelines, trapping us in an avalanche of our deepest, darkest memories.

Chapter Twenty

Erica,

You know, I did see you tonight.

Through the window of the trolley, I think. Or maybe at the Carl's Jr. parking lot. Speaking of weird, you looked so weird when I saw you through the window, like you were a ghost.

We're not talking now, but you still talked to me tonight. Thank you for that. It made me feel good again. And when I remembered you weren't talking to me, but realized you were talking to me, that's when I had to go.

I'm a little hungover right now. The notes app is so cool because you can talk into it and it types it out for you. I go back though sometimes and make the words sound good. I'm not hungover but burnt out. Strung out. Just being real with you. It is literally the worst, Erica. It's like when your entire energy is fading, the starlight is dimming, and the wishes you cast once upon a star are never going to come true.

I probably won't call you for a while. I know you're close, and I'm close to you, literally, but it feels like we're there again, floating in space, at two ends of the galaxy, calling out through the universe to each other but still missing our calls. You're leaving me on **READ**. Being ghosted by your own sister sucks.

Why are you doing this to me?

Is that all I am to you, Erica?

A ghost?

Some nights I want to say "duck you" to you. Autocorrect just fixed that. I will never say it to you, because I love you. But I do want to say that to you because you're doing this to me. You're leaving me to live in the shadows when you could just answer my freaking calls!

Why are you ignoring me?

You keep shutting me out.

You're doing this to me. And you're doing it on purpose.

We're not kids anymore, Erica.

You don't have to be like a little baby brat placing me in timeout for doing something bad! I'm almost thirty, sweet lord! But you treat me like I'm a little goo goo baby who wants a bottle. What the duck is wrong with you!

My phone put an exclamation mark after that. I didn't mean it as a statement but as a question. You are wrong, though, for just being so weird to me. I'm not being weird—you are. Stop saying that to me. I bet you're saying it right now after you saw me.

But it was you who came up to me. I didn't go up to you. I respected your space just like you should respect mine, and I was just there trying to get some food. I wanted a big fat ass juicy hammy, and you didn't even let me get that 'cuz I dropped it when the trolley came sloshing through like a witch! Now I have to go to sleep hungry. I have been so hungry. You have no idea what it's like to always be walking on the roads!

And what are you doing right now, sitting in that car, driving around like you're actually working a job? It is such. A. Joke. Working out of your own car driving making no money when I know you hate it! Why do you even still do it, driving? I know it makes you mad because you get treated like junk, but maybe that's because you deserve it!

Oh my.

I'm sorry.

I didn't mean to say that.

You deserve to be treated like the little pretty princess you are. Not sarcastically, *lol*. But you've gotta be nicer to people! Maybe if you just answer their freaking messages, maybe they'll be like, *oh hey, that's a cool Lyft driver, she actually responds to my messages,* and then you'll get more money and then you'll duck your future husband and die one day.

Got it. That's what life is. God. You're just going from stop to stop, moving between moments with the passengers of your car, pretending that you know where you're going when really, you're just going everywhere and nowhere, leading yourself to destinations you think you belong in.

But you're just fooling yourself, little princess.

You're not even working a real job.

You're just turning on your phone and opening an app and pressing a button. Where are you really going in your life? What are you building toward? And then you're driving. Going home. Sleeping. Doing it again. Just as stuck as you were years ago.

I became famous and got money.

You know, it's actually your own fault you're stuck there. You always told me, *oh, jeez, Dianne, this is such a hard job,* because people treat you worse than your waitress, and you always said that you can tell a lot about a person by the way they treat their Lyft driver. You said sometimes you weren't even there, in your own car.

But there you were, in the front seat, so sad and lonely and isolated and dealing with *de-press-ion* because sad little me was so *lost*, you claimed, *going to die*, you added, because people would enter into something that was yours and act as though you weren't even there, a ghost, and because you were already so lonely, this made you feel lonelier, and poor little baby Er-Bear, you're so down on yourself because of this!

I don't mean to sound like a brat either. You are working so hard and I am so proud of you. I love you, but I also hate you kind of for these things, for pretending that you're a ghost when really you're doing it to yourself.

Nobody is telling you that you have to be there.

Sweet lord. I'm really freaking high right now to be completely honest with you.

Dang.

It's not a high like *oh I'm out of this world* high; it's a hyper high like *oh I am controlling the world* high.

Or things within it.

But we really can't control anything, can we? We are just two little specks spinning on a planet spinning in the void, wandering aimlessly like your car on the streets, wheels spinning, teeth grinding, searching for purpose in the shadows when really, we're just objects floating in the middle of everywhere.

I saw you tonight, or last night, 'cuz it's maybe four in the morning, and wow the trolley is crossing but there's no one on it. I saw in the window—the itty bitty one above the big one—a certain kind of reflection, like someone from Old Town, San Diego, staring there, standing here, lost in time, a lonely wanderer riding the midnight train, hoping to find a way off but stuck in gravity, spinning.

She was there and then I blinked and she was gone again.

She kind of looked like you.

Dang, it's so amazing, the things you see if you let yourself see them. I believe the poetic way to say that is *when you finally open your eyes*, but who writes the rules? And when I saw you, even for like a sec, I felt like I had come back to life, at least for a moment. For only a moment, why do they say that, when I saw you, Erica, and I heard your voice, even though we weren't talking to each other and aren't anymore, but I heard your voice and there I was, a headlight in the deer's eyes like a dear. And I froze like I was caught getting out of timeout, you motherducker! Ahahahaha! Not *you* you, but it's a phrase. Got it? I love words. *Lololol.*

It was like I was trapped in that dead starlight for a lil teensy bit, and when I heard you, the light turned back on. It was the old you, the one who you were before you made me cry because if I didn't go to get help and get clean spick and span shiny clean then I would die, but joke's on you, witches! I'm alive as duck!

I'm literally breathing right now and the air feels so fresh, you have no idea how fresh it is actually, like the ocean and the stars melted and you're sipping in liquid light. I'm fresh with a *ph*, like a PhD doctor dude but like fat with a *ph*.

You used to think I was so cool.

I always got it from you, though, to be honest, like how I'm being real with you always from here on out. I am who you are but differently built because our blood is from the same parents but we were born at different times, so we are not the same person but you are who I am in my heart sometimes, I think.

So, there I was, just a few hours ago, here but there, neither where but nor, and I was just walking back and forth, right there on Friars Road, back to Carl's and then 7-Eleven, waiting for food and to see my dude show up. He was a little late and maybe I was getting antsy, but the ants in your pants dance starts when you don't have the drugs in your trance and I finally got them after you left. Teehee. Please don't tell anyone.

It was kind of like that game, *The Oregon Trail*, that we played, and I was just walking back and forth, back and forth, waiting to reach the other end of the trail and I saw you in the car tonight, I really did—at least I think I did, but I could also be imagining that, now that I think of it.

I think I can download the app of that game on my phone now. It would be so fun to have something to play when I'm here in the shadows.

It was cold and I felt like I was just walking on the same road, over and over again, but then you were there, and the starlight was back, even if it was the dead starlight that we had been so scared of as kids, but at least for a moment's moment you were there, and I didn't feel so lost.

But you left and then I did, too.

-Dianne

CHAPTER TWENTY-ONE

The world dissolved and I found myself floating in the Interstate, hovering between ghosts of memories. An infinite row of screens stretched before me, sparkling and flashing and restarting. I tried reaching out to stop myself from spinning, but as soon as I caught hold onto the pixels, my hands floated straight through.

I was caught between the future, the present, and the past. I was half dead, half alive, floating in limbo, searching desperately for a way out.

"Please. Make this stop." My voice echoed in reverb. "I can't do this any longer. My mind is playing tricks on me and I'm scared and I need to get back home."

Somewhere, mirrors and realms away, I heard Macy call to me from beyond.

"Erica…"

"Macy, I'm right here!" I swam in place, following the sound of her voice. "Where are you?"

I somersaulted through a stream of endless mirrors, steering myself in the direction of her memories. At last I saw the faint outline of Macy spiraling through the darkness. The ectoplasm swirling around her body was dimming. She turned my way, but it looked as though she was seeing right through me.

"It appears that I am caught in a death loop, and I cannot pull myself out. It is torture, Erica. I cannot stand to see my parents die again."

"I can't imagine what you must be feeling. It's like how Dianne is, well, losing herself in Bloody Mary's grasp. We'll find a way out, even if we can't do it together. Can you see me?"

"I can sense your presence, yes. Right now, I am hovering in that darkness between stars, in the place where memories go to die, except now I am the memory that is dying…"

"There must be something I can do to help. I'll do anything to get us out. What's really happening to us?"

"Bloody Mary is growing stronger. Every time that we neuroflash back in time and let her distort our identities, we are powering the ectoplasm that fuels her spirit. If we do not enter into her end of the mirror and stop her from rewriting these moments soon, then there is a chance we will be stuck here, forever, just as she is. And if that happens, all you will see in the mirror, is her. We will essentially be erased, too."

"I won't let that happen, Macy. I won't let you, or us, be trapped here any longer. I will never let her erase Dianne's story."

Macy opened her mouth to speak, but before she could say another word, she disappeared into the darkness.

Though my body was dimmer, I summoned the neuroflash in my skull and tumbled through the screen.

~ ~ ~

When I jolted out of the neuroflash, I found myself living the memory of the day of my Senior Prom. Dianne had already happily agreed to help me prepare for the night, so re-experiencing this entire day with her from the very start of the morning, when she took me to Starbucks, would be such a treasure.

During most of my high school years, I would've been lost without her. Sometimes, I'd be wandering around the lunch area, searching for a table that would feel right to sit at. High school was so stupidly cliquey. If I wasn't sitting with the Drama Club kids, I'd be somewhere halfway between sitting under a staircase or hiding in the library, pretending to study.

Because Dianne and I were in high school choir together, we luckily had some extracurricular club activities taking place during lunch, so at least I had somewhere to hide. But it was because Dianne was there, and maybe she knew it, too. Maybe that's even why she joined the club, so I would have an excuse to see her during the day. Even though I gave her the space that she needed at school, I always found myself gravitating toward her, because she was my sister.

I was doing what any younger siblings would do, really. I loved her more than she could have known. She reminded me of who I wanted to become, of who I could be, if I kept pushing through the harder moments of high school.

She never knew just how much of a rock she was to me during those years, when my anxiety and depression started manifesting in ways I never could have imagined. And during those times, I didn't know that's what I was experiencing. It was lying dormant, waiting to catch up with me when things turned south with Dianne. High school could be a lonely place, and my life felt like it was spiraling out of control. It was easier knowing she was there, a classroom away, if I ever needed her.

Now, in my revisit of Senior Prom, the day felt like one of those dreams I never wanted to wake up from. I was going to spend an entire day with my deceased sister, and though I possessed the knowledge that I held before I'd flashed here, I started to lose myself in the moment. I swear I almost forgot I neuroflashed here. It was as if today was *actually* today.

My boyfriend at the time, Dylan, was going to meet at our house right around six. So, Dianne had already planned to spend the day with me as I prepared for prom, just the two of us. We went to a nail salon in the morning, got our hair done at the Fashion Valley Mall in the afternoon, and did our makeup in the late afternoon. Today, it was the smaller things that meant the most to me. A cliché description to use, maybe, but it was true. When you're experiencing small moments with someone you know will not be there tomorrow, it becomes truer than you can ever believe.

What happened next kind of sucked, though. Long story short, my date never showed up. Apparently, he had pre-gamed so much to the point where he wasn't able to drive. We were both eighteen and he didn't know his tolerance, and, honestly, he never should have gone that hard, ever. We obviously didn't have Lyft and Uber back then, so he was gone, completely out of the picture. I never forgave him for it, and after high school, I never checked up on him on Facebook or anywhere, really. I pretty much stopped thinking about him.

But that day when he stood me up in the past, and now, it was torture. Even knowing that I would be okay, I couldn't speed up this memory. I had to relive every aspect of it. I stood there watching helplessly as my friends' dates all showed up, each pairing off with each other. My heart sank as I waited for who I thought was supposed to be my forever high school sweetheart to show up.

My friends were very understanding and insisted that I just keep waiting a little longer. They all reassured me that he'd show up. He was the head of the ASB. He had to at least show his face at the dance if he wanted to win Prom King.

It was a quarter to seven. We needed to get to school soon if we were to make the 7:15 cutoff. I didn't know why the school had instilled that rule, but I think they wanted to ward off anyone like Dylan who had decided to get trashed before the dance. My friends made the limo driver wait, but even his patience started wearing thin.

Dianne had been watching through the window. She knew what was happening.

"Hey, Er-Bear." The door opened, and she stood in the doorway, standing in the same purple gown she had worn two years ago to her own prom. "Looks like your date showed up."

"My date?"

She cleared her throat and pointed both of her thumbs to her chest.

"Wait, what?" I said.

"You know, your date? A.k.a., the coolest date on the face of the Earth?"

I gasped. I hadn't realized she could be that cool.

"Really? You'd do that for me?"

She nodded and smiled. It never stood out to me in that moment, but her smile literally brightened up the room, shining through the air around her, as though the ectoplasm shone through her body, too.

"Come on. Let's get this party started already."

"No way."

"Yep. I'm coming with, no *ifs*, *ands*, or *buts*. I mean, who else would you want to go with?"

I gave her one of those bear hugs. I couldn't help myself. There she was, saving the day for me again, like she always did. But that was simply the type of person she was—caring, protective, and kind. She always went the extra mile, even when she had nothing in it for herself. Sometimes, it even seemed as though she placed my happiness above hers.

Arm in arm, we stepped into that long suburban limo truck and rode off to prom, together.

Twinkling lights lined the limo's ceiling. We drank cream soda and we laughed as we watched the fake stars twinkle above us. We joined in the dance party as everyone started doing the Soulja Boy. It really was the small things that mattered.

I did everything I possibly could to keep from crying. I did not want to draw any more attention to myself. I wouldn't see any of them after this. My brain tried to comprehend where I was, who I was with, and how I was reacting, but soon my thoughts shifted to the music, Dianne's laughter, and the stars above, and I truly lost myself in the moment.

For the first time in forever, I felt like I was alive.

We pulled up to Northwater High School's parking lot and stepped out of the limo like we were walking up to a red carpet. With Dianne, it always felt that way, because she lit up the world's stage with every step she took.

We danced through the night.

I never wanted to leave this moment.

I wanted it to last forever.

But it couldn't.

So, I cherished the moment as she slow-danced with me at the end of the night. When the limo dropped us off at the afterparty, she requested we be dropped off at home instead.

She said forget it, let's just go to Carl's Jr.

She drove me there, and I started crying, knowing it would be one of the last times I would see her like this, and she asked why I was sad, and I told her it was because of Dylan. But I didn't tell her it was because she was there but she *wasn't* there, and she would never know how hard it was to order French fries as I started seeing the ectoplasm in the rearview mirror, ready to pull me through.

But I held on a little longer. Even if Mary's reflections disturbed this moment somehow, I wouldn't allow my neuroflash to activate. I needed to spend time with her. There was some deeper reason why we were here, again, in this moment.

We drove to the park, lay on the grass, and counted the stars. They seemed to be shining brighter than I remembered, but maybe it was because I had seen the ectoplasm, and knew what these memories were made of.

"Dianne?" I asked, finishing the last bite of my cookie. "Can I ask you something?"

"Of course."

"Were you ever scared when you were my age? You know, of life after high school, college, life in general, all that good stuff?"

She smiled and slurped her ice cream smoothie. "Yeah, of course. All the time. Didn't we have this conversation before, when we were kids?"

"Does it ever go away?"

"You mean, like, worrying about stuff, or being afraid of college? 'Cuz that will pass, too, obviously."

"No, I mean, this sounds so stupid. I'm going to sound pretty pathetic. But…what if all we had was this moment? What if the only thing that mattered was right now, before it goes away?"

Somewhere in the sky, a satellite rushed by. Or it could've been a shooting star. I was so lost in the moment that I didn't really care either way. I made a wish, knowing it most likely wouldn't come true.

"I mean, yeah. Sure. I still get scared of what's next. I have no idea what happens after today. No one does, really."

"Do you think there's a reason we're alive, you know, if we're just going to die someday?"

Dianne inhaled her cookie and started coughing. She laughed so loudly that it echoed through the empty playground. Then, she was silent.

"Oh, you're serious."

"Kind of."

"Okay. That's okay. I swear, you haven't changed one bit. Like I said back then, it's normal to think that way. I just wasn't prepared for you to talk about the hard stuff. Everything okay?"

"Sorry. I didn't mean for it to…" I trailed off as I thought of the future, of seeing those tabloid news reports, of seeing her at that same Carl's Jr., the empty, dead look in her eyes as she looked through me, after the dead stars had eaten her. "Dianne. Do things really matter?"

"What things?"

"You know. Spending time together, and stuff?" She nodded. "And then we're gone?"

She didn't answer for a moment, her eyes fixed on the sky above.

"Probably. Maybe we go somewhere. I hope we do."

"I do, too."

In that moment, something else filled her eyes. The reflection of something terrifying. When she spoke, her voice was dowsed in reverb, as though shouting to me through the void. Bloody Mary's reflections were somewhere in the park, waiting for us in the shadows.

"And when I go to that place, I hope I'll see you there, too."

It was Mary's voice.

A sudden dread filled me, pumping through my body. The sky seemed to fall upon me, a weight growing on my chest. The memories we had shared, and the memories we would become, had been prewritten by Bloody Mary all along. Were we ever here to begin with? We were pretending to chase out our destinies, when, really, we were trapped there, within the mirror.

The shadows were waiting somewhere, preparing to strike. I tried manifesting ectoplasm, but I couldn't channel the power of that starlight and the memories that I needed to save like I used to. I was losing strength.

I started sobbing.

Back then, Dianne might not have known the significance of this moment, or why I cried so hard during her momentary possession. She was only a puppet, unaware that she had fallen into Bloody Mary's grasp.

And then Bloody Mary's reflection swirled in her eyes. She manifested as shadows, burrowing under Dianne's pupils like termites, slithering under the whites of her eyes until her face slammed against their surfaces.

"Ew!" Dianne screamed, slapping at her eyelids. "Erica! I think there's a bug in my eye."

"Don't move. You're making it worse." I had to pretend it would all go away. That was the only way she would have comprehended it in the past. But I needed to think. I wouldn't let Bloody Mary rewrite this moment. I couldn't let her continue to possess Dianne and take control of her identity.

So I stood and stared deeply into Dianne's eyes. If I couldn't yet enter into Bloody Mary's mirror, then I needed to be as physically close to her as humanly possible to feel the power of her essence. I needed my reflection to discover the trail of memories that led to her mirror. It was the only thing I could do as I focused on recharging the ectoplasm in my veins. I stood my ground as my entire world was about to collapse.

"Bloody Mary, I know you're in there. And, yeah, I'm not afraid to say your name any longer. I can see you, right there, trying to rewrite this very moment." Dianne looked at me, confused. The air shifted and time seemed to stretch a little longer. "I know you are trying to possess my sister, but now, I won't let you."

"And what makes you think you can do that?" Dianne's eyes rolled into her head as Bloody Mary's voice seeped through her mouth. "What makes you think you are brave enough to face me in the mirror?"

"Because while I was afraid back then, Bloody Mary, I'm not any longer."

"How very courageous of you, Erica. But who do you think I am? Are you truly brave enough to see?" Dianne stood in a trance and walked towards the park playground. She laughed. It was a demonic chuckle, tripled in clashing harmony with overtones of the spirits Bloody Mary had killed ages ago.

Dianne's eyes shot wide open and tears started streaming down her face. Bloody Mary dripped down her chin, morphing into a ghastly ectoplasm that surrounded Dianne's body in a thick, crimson mist.

"Can you see me now, Erica? What do I look like?" Bloody Mary raised Dianne's arms. Ectoplasm sparked from her fingertips. "Do I look like your dead sister? Do I look like everyone who has ever lived and died? Go on, tell me."

Bloody Mary flew in the air and shot a beam of ectoplasm straight at my head.

I ducked and rolled underneath the plastic slide as the bolt of light landed behind me. A plume of sand mixed with ectoplasm rained onto the playground, covering the park in a haze of dirt and memories.

I crawled underneath the slide's staircase and caught my breath. I needed to focus on the present, in the past, while forgetting about my future. It was almost impossible. But the only way I could transcend Bloody Mary's mirror was to understand the power contained within her reflection.

I needed to forget who I was.

Bloody Mary shot through the monkey bars and hovered in mid-air, studying me.

"Who do you think you are, Erica Westfield?"

"I don't know who I will become, but with Dianne in my life, I know who I've wanted to be." Starlight channeled through my veins. The neuroflash chimed at the center of my mind. My veins sparkled. "And if I can be anything like her, then there is nothing to be afraid of."

I started lifting into the air, propelled by the ectoplasm shining at my fingertips. My feet dragged across the sand as the world spun around me. I flew, and suddenly, I was no longer hovering solely in the past.

I was living in three dimensions at once—the past, the present, and the future, unafraid of the memories I would create beyond the Interstate.

For a moment, Bloody Mary looked frightened. As I soared to her, she hovered backwards, retreating behind the monkey bars. She was afraid of the starlight that shone in my blood.

Somewhere beneath Bloody Mary's hovering spirit, something was shifting within Dianne. I couldn't put my finger on it, but she seemed more aware of her surroundings, as though she was no longer just a living memory. It was her spirit, manifesting into the ghost of her past life, calling out through the distant mirror reflected in her eyes from realms away.

I reached out to Dianne, hoping to catch hold of her sentient soul, urging her to wake up, but as soon as I did, my hand just slipped through hers.

"I have secrets to share with you, Erica." Bloody Mary's crimson ectoplasm dripped from my fingertips and crawled up my arms. "Do you wish to attain this knowledge?"

I screamed as the dead memories contained within Bloody Mary's spirit inched through my veins.

A sudden sense of depression overtook me. I couldn't run away from it, now. If I wanted to save Dianne's spirit, I had to make peace with the terror that awaited me, there, in a world I would have to endure without her. I needed to give into this feeling. I needed to feel the emptiness that had overtaken me after I had heard of Dianne's death.

I found myself there, in my head, in that dead place between the stars.

I lost myself in the shadows of my skull and let them take hold of me.

"You really loved her, didn't you? But your sister is dead, Erica. You and I both know that. There is nothing you can do to fight the future from happening. I can erase the memories after this moment, and you can live here, forever, where she is alive. But it would have to come with a price. Give me her spirit, and I will let yours go."

"I couldn't save her when I was alive, Bloody Mary. I couldn't save her from her addiction." The ectoplasm stormed from my fingertips and reflected brilliantly in her terrified eyes. The light shifted between hues of blood-red, gold, purple, and silver. The colors of the universe shone around me as my memories blurred with Bloody Mary's. "But now, I still might have a chance. I will never let you take my sister's soul, not when she can find peace in a place where she will remember who she has been."

I charged to Bloody Mary and blasted a beam of ectoplasm straight at her chest.

She squealed as the cosmic light tore through her, a swirl of gold and violet and red erupting from her chest.

The force of the light knocked her backwards through the monkey bars to the slide, leaving blips and pixels of dead memories in her wake.

I flew to the top of the plastic playground, perching on the roof, aiming my hands toward her heart.

"Oh, Erica." She shook her head. "You will never be strong enough to travel through *my* mirror. But if you think you're ready, then we'll have a little fun. Be prepared to face your deepest, darkest demons."

She transformed into a beam of light and catapulted into the air, leaving Dianne sitting on the playground slide. I flew down to her as my ectoplasm dimmed.

As I helped Dianne come to her senses, Bloody Mary was a mere shooting star in the dead of night. I watched in sick wonder as a trail of crystal memories flowed behind her until she disappeared into the horizon.

I felt the neuroflash glimmer at the edge of mind. I had to travel further through the dead memories Bloody Mary had just injected into me in order to save Dianne's spirit. I hugged my sister there in the past, and then I wished presently that she could come with me, but when I wished upon that bleeding shooting star in the night sky for the things I knew would not come true, I neuroflashed through the void, deeper into the Interstate, folding back into myself.

CHAPTER TWENTY-TWO

Hey, Erica,

You didn't have to block me again. I didn't ever mean for us to get to that point. I don't think anyone ever does. I hope I didn't come across as angry. I'm just trying to sort things out.

I know you'll never read this, because I'll never send this to you, but I'll send it to myself here on my Messenger, just for good measure. It might help me process everything. "Process" sounds like such a cold word, though, like processing things through a computer. Which, I guess, technically I am. Aren't we all, nowadays?

Sometimes, when I type the words out, especially here online, they make everything feel more real, like I'm actually connecting with someone else. Isn't that strange? Even if no one reads this, at least the words have been here, right now, in this moment, or whenever I'll press send, if I ever do. Kind of like a song, I suppose. I hope you can read this with the melody of my voice sometime in the future.

Then this message will be like that dead starlight.

A strange, cosmic time capsule. You'll hear the past version of myself when this gets to you, even though I'm the "right now" version of me. Trippy, bro. Real trippy. *Lol.*

I know you were scared of a lot of things, but that was one of them, the space between the stars. That big no-man's land of nothingness, a portal to nowhere. You weren't scared, necessarily, but you were fascinated in a terrified kind of way. Was it weird to be thinking about death so much? I mean, I know we all do, but to think about it so much to the point where you're afraid of the shadows, that's when I got worried about you.

When we were just little kids, wee tykes, little lasses, you told me of the shadows that we conjured up that night, looking into the mirror, playing that stupid game that we should've stayed far away from. I don't mean to call it stupid, because I don't want you to think I'm diminishing your trauma whatsoever. But you said you saw something like ectoplasm? Or star shine, the starlight that was dead but was still shining onto us?

I'm sorry. I should have given you a trigger warning before bringing that up. Maybe I'll just delete that section entirely, or reshape it to find a softer way of saying it. But also, I want to be real with you, because you're my sister, Erica. My Er-Bear. But I hope that by now, it's become less painful to think about. I know we talked about it a bunch of times, and you seem to be doing really, really good overall. I'm super proud of you, I really am.

Remember, that night, though, when I went to your prom after you got stood up by that lame-ass guy? What was his name again? I could tell he'd turn out to be a real frat-bro once he got to college. I'm glad it never worked out between you too, just being real again. Anyways, we were lying on the grass, and we were looking at the night sky, and we couldn't really see the stars, being in the middle of the suburbs and all, but we pretended we could, and we could see some of them, which was cool, and then we talked about some pretty heavy stuff.

You got really sad for a moment, like really, really sad. I'd never seen you start to cry so hard out of nowhere. I know it wasn't out of nowhere, because some things just get bottled up over time. Honestly, I thought I had said something wrong to you. You might not have known it then, but I didn't really know what I was saying, either. Anytime you'd ask serious questions, I'd always pretend to know the right thing to say, just to make sure you were okay. I wasn't lying to you ever, except about the drug stuff, but I got really worried for a sec, too, because we were having such an awesome night, and I didn't want to take anything away from that.

We were looking at the stars, and you asked if that was the only moment we would have, if there was anything on the other side.

I didn't know if you were talking about the other side of the stars, or space, or not. I like to believe we're not alone, that there's something watching over us, all that good stuff. I might have said something that made me sound like I actually knew what I was talking about, but the truth is, I never really knew.

You were scared of telling me how you felt because you thought I would become afraid of you for thinking those things. It's so funny how our minds work.

I didn't know what to say at the time. I just pretended that there was a shooting star soaring past us, even though it was probably just an airplane, but what you didn't know was, I did wish for something, even though I didn't know if it was real or not.

I wished that you would be okay.

It sounds vague, and it sounds kind of funny to say this, but in that moment, it actually felt real. Like the wish came true. And it wasn't a wish just for that moment, but for everything that would come your way in the future.

Because when you hugged me, I got the weirdest feeling. It was kind of like déjà vu, almost as though we hadn't seen each other for years and you were finally hugging me after so long. Like we had been stuck at two opposite sides of the galaxy, floating between the stars, and when I hugged you back, I felt like the starlight had finally come back because you were shining onto me and I could hear it in the way you were crying and I was trying so hard not to cry, too.

It was a real moment for me.

Does that make sense?

There are some moments we've shared together where it's felt like more than just a moment. Not to sound redundant, but those moments made life worth living. It was like we were in a memory we were acting out in real time, because you told me everything I needed to hear, word for word, and I would tell you everything you needed to hear, and we were just like two stars, then, shining at opposite ends of the universe, reminding each other we'd be okay, trying to contemplate why things on our own timelines didn't feel right.

But you provided me with infinite starshine. You lit up my life in ways you never could have known. It's crazy, if you really think about it, that some of the stars lighting up this night's sky might be dead. I don't mean that to sound morbid, but how is it possible that when something can provide a light so bright, it can literally transcend space and time? Here we are, looking up, going, *ahh, yes, what a beautiful night*, but that night might be both dead and alive, stuck in limbo, eternally.

We are alive now, and maybe, one day, that dead starshine won't scare us.

But it does scare me.

We shared so many amazing moments, Erica. I hope to turn things around so I can experience many more with you. Things have been hard. I know keeping our distance is intentional, and at this point, it's my fault. I'll admit it. It feels good to think about these types of things. In fact, maybe I discovered that just by typing this out. I wanna stay sober, not just for me, but for you, too, and for those memories we'll be able to make someday, together.

I know that I have a lot of work to do. I've gotten pretty low, but right now, I'm here, sitting behind my computer, my monitor, my mirror, in a new apartment I got a few months before the pandemic. I think I can use this as an opportunity to finally get some writing done. Maybe I'll even write a song about you.

I hope that when you see this message, I can reflect back on this moment and say, yeah, things turned out okay.

I know they will, though, because my wish came true that night, when I wished upon a dead star.

I love you, Erica.

-Dianne

CHAPTER TWENTY-THREE

The next thing I knew, Erica, I neuroflashed back to the past, propelled by the knowledge of the future, possessed with the context of hindsight.

My life flashed before my eyes as the ectoplasm around my body diminished to a soft glow. I found myself standing outside of the wagon again, next to Father.

I had flashed back to that moment again, right before they were about to die. Perhaps I had even been here many times before.

It was cruel. They were waiting for us, somewhere in the shadows. I couldn't take it anymore. I had to do something about it.

"Father?"

"Macy?" He blinked, tears streaming down his face. There were more wrinkles around his eyes than I remembered. When he had previously learned of the gold that was possibly waiting for us in California, he'd had a sparkle in his eyes, as though he really did know what was waiting for us there on the other side. But now, he looked older, his face weathered like a soldier who had returned from battle.

"Macy." He repeated this as though answering a question. A certain kind of understanding flickered in his eyes. He must have known where I had just been, what monsters I had faced, the terrors lurking beyond the other side of my mirror. Did he know, though, that I had seen him die, over and over?

I didn't need to explain it to him. He must have had some type of deep intuition, an unspoken sixth sense, because that look in his eyes said it all. Though he might have not been mortally aware, something deep within his spirit knew.

I gave him the biggest hug I could. I didn't want to let go. Though I had lived this memory before, this was the only moment I really had.

Because they were waiting for us in the memories yet to be written.

"This locket… Father, please, tell me what is inside it."

"My dear Macy." He held the locket in his hands, his cold fingers leaving frosty prints on its metal lining. "You remember, then. We have been here before, have we not? You have seen the life beyond ours, through the looking glass."

"Yes. I have been here before, Father. Tell me. How do I break out of this?"

"I do not have the answer to that." He frowned and let the locket sway in the wind. "But if you hold onto hope, the answer will become clearer. As you see your life flash before your eyes, Macy, you will see something else there, far past the horizon, where spirits know no bounds, where knowledge knows no words. Once you stare into the power of infinity, you will understand how to contain it."

"Contain it?"

Father nodded. "You might not believe it, but this trail we are traveling in our lives does not only have one other end to it."

A glimmer of a smile lit up the corner of his lips. Though we were freezing in the midnight air, I couldn't help but feel a certain warmth spread in my heart. It was nice to see Father happy, even for a brief moment.

"There is this life, the one we comprehend here, in our hearts," he continued, "and there is the reflection of it, death, the one we will understand there, one day, in our souls. But there is something else, too. An *afterlife*. A life that can be relived in any moment one chooses, forever."

"Am I there now? Your riddles mean nothing, Father. Tell me what you have been hiding."

"Though I have stared into the stars, I have not seen what you have seen, and therefore, I cannot tell you what you wish to know. But this eternal life I have spoken of, somewhere in the starlight—there is also another place, where there is nothing. It is a place of death that exists between two beacons of light. It is an invisible trail, a distorted reflection of starlight, that links two entities together. If one star is plagued by evil forces within this energy force, then both of these stars will potentially fade until they shine no longer. If this power to relive any moment is misused, then a soul can become stuck there, traveling endlessly between stars, searching for the trail back to their memories, where they wish to shine again."

He held the locket and pointed the mirror towards my face.

"Macy, your Mother and I know that you are special. You are the greatest gift we have ever received from the universe. Tell me, who do you see staring back at you, now?"

He wavered the mirror in the night sky. Behind me, in the looking glass, I became a silhouette in the starlight. For a moment, I was floating within my own universe.

"I see someone who is afraid of the future."

"What else do you see?"

"I see someone who was hurt by the past."

"And what else?"

I shrugged. "I don't quite know who I see yet, Father. But I know who I want to become. I want to be like you, and Mother, and Bessie. Except I am not sure how that will work out, because I don't have hooves." Father laughed. "I don't know, Father. I am just a child. I do not want to leave this life before I have the chance to create these memories you speak of."

"I see someone else. Someone who possess infinite strength. Throughout your life, the person you see staring back at you in the mirror will change. You have choices in this mortal life that will test your ability to hold onto hope. They will reveal to you the infinite power that your spirit contains. But also, if you are reliving your worst memories, there, in this dead place, you have the capacity to understand the power of infinite hope, in every desperate moment you face."

Father closed the locket and placed it into my hands.

"You are a gift, Macy, but you are also a weapon. You are a collection of memories, a star shining brilliant light into our lives. The light you possess can help fight off these evil forces that live there, in that dead place. I do not know if you are there, Macy, but if you are, then you might have the chance to help others back on their trail, to the other side, wherever that might be in their lives. If you hold onto hope, and help others hold onto it, then that is how we will all get to the other end of this trail."

I was about to hug Father, to tell him that although I had seen him die a thousand times, the pain in these memories didn't matter anymore, because I was there with him, now, in this very moment. But in the reflection of his eyes, I saw Bloody Mary and her reflections creeping through the shadows. I couldn't do a thing to stop them, just like I couldn't the last time. I could not feel the warmth of the starlight to channel the ectoplasm in my soul. I could not remember the memories that waited for me there, on the other side.

I did what Father told me to. It was the only thing I could do. I held onto hope, desperately, as they killed Mother and Father again.

I fell into Bloody Mary's locket, neuroflashing to somewhere in the future.

CHAPTER TWENTY-FOUR

Macy, please. Help me.

I'm trapped now, here in these memories upon memories that Bloody Mary has poisoned me with. I am losing the light, just like you are. The ectoplasm is quickly fading through my skin, and I am afraid that I will be stuck here, forever, like you have been stuck there, forever, on the other side.

If you can hear me, pull me out of this.

I need to go back home to my apartment. I need to take a break. I need to sleep because this is too much for me and I can't relive this moment, especially right now, because I have just lived the moment after this moment and I can't do this, Macy, I can't do this anymore.

~ ~ ~

I had just neuroflashed through my phone's screen to my car, tumbling forward into another memory.

This might have been, in retrospect, the worst night of my life, although I didn't know it at the time.

I definitely knew it now.

It was 12:14 a.m., that reflective hour yet again. I was sitting in a Taco Bell parking lot in Newport Beach, California, working Lyft and Uber. I had a ride that brought me all the way down here, and now I was waiting for another ride to take me back home to San Diego, hopefully compensating for the gas money, although that rarely happened. I should add that I was also working Postmates and Uber Eats, so I was essentially hopping between three and a half jobs while running on empty, both with my gas tank and my energy levels.

I was about to make the extra hundred bucks that would allow me to pay rent if I waited, just a little longer. My Grubhub application still had not gone through, so I was doing anything I could to make money and take my mind off the fact that Dianne had been trying to message me again on Facebook. I sat there in the semi-darkness, a streetlight strobing on and off in the distance. If ghosts could tamper with lights, then maybe it was actually me who was causing this shortage of electricity.

I downed my Red Bull. I needed to stay awake for at least another three hours. Two to allow an extra passenger ride back home, one to hopefully watch some mindless reality TV. Lately, Dianne had been in one of her manic phases again, induced by who-knew-what drug. Last I heard, she had moved to heavier substances. Though I had blocked her main account, she had created another one, and I blocked that one, too, and then another one, and I also blocked that one, and then it became too much for me, so I stopped going on Facebook altogether.

I had basically disappeared from social media. I had *liked* people's statuses and had replied to comments when people tagged me, but the last major life update I did was right after Dianne came back from her first tour.

That was when she had become someone else.

After that, I had posted that I was going to take a year off from school. I posted that I was shifting some things in my life around, although I never revealed what exactly. It was one of those vague posts that made people leave a comment along the lines of, "Proud of you, Erica, for chasing after your dreams," even though I had no idea what my dreams could still be after seeing how hard Dianne had fallen.

What I really wanted to post was, "My sister is hurting, and because she is hurting, I am hurting, and I need to be there for her so she will be okay." But that would have elicited a lot of drama, and interventions left in the open weren't really interventions. They were just surprise attacks that weren't a surprise at all, and they wouldn't work, not unless they were organic.

I wanted to reveal everything right there and then, on my phone, to compensate for the amount of times I hadn't posted in the past year. I wanted to tell everyone that I was currently sitting in an empty Taco Bell parking lot, trying to make some money while being a gig worker, waiting for opportunities that might never come, about how I was really close to just crying again, but it made me feel so pathetic, so I resisted. Then I thought that maybe I could disguise it with a post telling my friends that they should tell me about the moment when we first met, to see who I might be able to call upon when I was hurting, but that would also be really vague and wouldn't get the message across.

Although everyone was there, right on my timeline, it also seemed like a ghost town. People were moving on with their lives. I was stuck here, in this empty parking lot, me and my unattainable dreams flashing by.

It felt like I was living in a simulation. No matter how many times I tried pulling myself out of this situation, out of this endless loop of driving around aimlessly through the night, barely making any money to get by, I found myself here, yet again, in an empty parking lot, crying out to the Twitterverse for something, someone, to help pull me through.

In reality, it was just yesterday when this happened.

I was still living in this memory loop. Before I had even entered into the Interstate, floating alongside Macy, propelled into my own memories through the neuroflash, I was already stuck in an endless cycle of memories, of being alive yet not feeling alive, hovering in my own limbo between the millennial late-twenties adolescence and adulthood.

I had everything to say, and yet, I had nothing to say.

I was living in a paradox of life, of existing and withdrawing from the endless pain of this cycle of depression.

So, I didn't post anything.

As I stared at my phone, thinking of posting about nothing, I got a text.

A text from Dianne.

My heart did that thing again where it felt like butterflies exploding in my stomach. It was the trigger of all triggers, an instant pain that shot throughout my entire body. It was more than a flight-or-flight response—it was a cloud of my own personal demons resurfacing out of nowhere on my phone.

She was texting me from a new number now.

I took a deep breath.

I couldn't read it.

But I did.

All the text said was: *Hey, hey, Erica, I'm blasting through the portal, you know what I mean?*

I was about to block the number when she sent another text.

Please help me.

Help me.

Erica.

Why are you not here?

I'm hurting.

I couldn't reply. She had done this at least twenty times before, but texting me from a new number was different. She was just texting me, though, because my number was one of the only ones she remembered off the top of her head. She was just doing anything in her current mental state that made sense. Isn't that funny, how we remember some things, and yet we can't remember what we ate for breakfast five days ago? Even in her drug-fueled state, she knew my number inside and out, whether she was texting me from someone else's phone or not.

I kept telling myself to just keep waiting for another ride, and once I got a ride then I would block the number and pretend to slap on a smile to hopefully make some money during primetime for an hour-long ride. I needed the money. I couldn't do this anymore. I was emotionally and physically and spiritually exhausted.

Then she called me.

I didn't pick up.

I couldn't hear her like that.

She sent another series of messages. I read these texts as they came in. They weren't complete sentences, so I was able to read them without opening them. I was able to distance myself from the situation with one extra layer of defense, at least virtually. I would leave them unread even though I was reading them. It hurt less that way.

Erica.

Er-bear.

I'm.

I'm sorry.

I didn't mean to.

Put you through this.

Tonight.

I will call you.

Please.

Please answer.

I love you.

Very very much!!!!!!!!!

She called me again.

I let it pass.

And again.

I didn't answer.

If I did, I would have broken down right there and then, and then I wouldn't have the strength to drive back home. I would have had to sleep in the Taco Bell parking lot to make sure I would get home safely.

I was sure that Dianne would forgive me, once she sobered up.

And then one last series of texts came through.

I love you, Er-Bear.

You are my person.

Please forgive me.

The trigger flowed through me again. It wasn't Dianne who was sending these messages. Bloody Mary had possessed her all along. I knew it in my heart. Bloody Mary made her forget her reflection, and now Dianne couldn't see herself in the mirror as she downed the pills. I needed to stop her from destroying these memories.

I was close to doing that sobbing thing that happened when I got really sad. Experiencing this moment, right now, presently, was just too much for me, knowing that she would end up dead that very night.

I felt the neuroflash strengthen in my heart. Bloody Mary was nearby, somewhere. I had a chance to put an end to Dianne's misery.

I was floating between these moments from within, like a mirror infinitely reflecting upon myself.

I closed my apps, turned off my phone, and drove home, just like I did that night, knowing she would die, not knowing, but knowing, and yet, I knew I could do something to still save her now, back there, in the past.

I summoned a neuroflash and felt myself lifting into the sky. I knew what I needed to do to break us all out of the Interstate.

I wouldn't just travel through Bloody Mary's mirror.

I would become her reflection.

And everything it contained.

CHAPTER TWENTY-FIVE

I tumbled through the Interstate, Erica, through the static Wi-Fi and algorithms and memories swirling around me in a delirious frenzy.

I fell out of the locket and found myself standing on the outskirts of a village. Without the ectoplasm guiding my way, I was lost. In a sense, I could see the stars but I couldn't identify the constellations. The planets were above me but I was no longer standing on solid ground. I was lost somewhere, floating in the void, the energy not only drained from my soul, but from the universe itself. The dead starlight had reflected onto something else now—Bloody Mary's mirror—and I needed to do anything to reflect it back into the sky, where it would become a memory that would hopefully die.

I had taken something from the stars, Erica, and I needed to give it back, if I were to ever find my place in this world again. I was growing tired. I could not see Mother and Father die again. I just couldn't.

But I was helpless to the trajectory of my destiny. Bloody Mary stepped out of the shadows, the faint moonlight shining through her transparent skin. She pointed toward the village that stood about a hundred feet away. As she lifted her arm, her reflections followed suit. Those hollowed, walking corpses in my previous memories lifted their skeletal fingers and stood in a circle around her. They had grown even more vile than before. It was almost as though within each memory, they evolved exponentially, transforming into the vilest creatures that had ever walked the Earth.

A resonating hum chimed in the air as they manifested ectoplasm from their fingertips, channeling the power of the dead starlight. The light pooled together, peeling back layers of the atmosphere until it burrowed into their skin, almost as though the sky was tearing itself apart.

Their bodies shifted before my very eyes, morphing into something like human beings. Bloody Mary looked like Marty again, and I wondered if the Marty I had come to know had ever been truly evil to begin with. Maybe she had raised him from the dead in another lifetime, just as I had raised many innocent lives as well. Though they could fool others, they couldn't fool me, because I could see it in their eyes.

It was the way the moonlight shone through their pupils. Erica, when somebody's eyes light up with joy, you can tell that there is much more to the body than just blood and bone. There is something inside every human being, somewhere deep inside, that reveals our humanity. Some call it a spirit; others call it a soul or a life force. However you classify it, you know it is there, this thing that makes us alive. If we are living, then we are gifted with that miracle of light within our hearts.

If eyes are windows to the soul, then the windows of their eyes truly led to nowhere. Their eyes were hollow, lifeless, full of wickedness, seeking any opportunity to claim the light of the living to feed the shadows that had eclipsed their souls. Their eyes were a window to the underworld, a place long forgotten, ancient, a blasphemy of the goodness that surrounds us, all shaped and molded by the hands of Bloody Mary herself.

I tried to look away, but I couldn't. I simply could not escape their eyes. If Bloody Mary had a hold on me, both then and now, this was how she operated. Within their eyes, I saw no reflection, and that reflection of nothingness reflected in my eyes infinitely. It made me forget who I was.

But I had to remember. I had traveled so far just to forget. I tried not to think of everything I had lost…my parents, my sweet, dear Bessie, and all of the other families who had died along the way. And yet, there I was, nearly on the other side of this trail that I had been trapped in. That long-fabled light shone at the end of the tunnel, just a few hundred feet away from me.

For a moment, it almost felt like an accomplishment. Something like warmth filled me, or happiness, or a fleeting moment of contentedness. In the distance, laughter echoed through the wintry tundra. On the other side of this town, an old man was whistling as he chipped away at the day's work, bringing logs to a fire. Daily life seemed to be what I remembered it to be, back in Oregon, before the new normal tore through my life. Perhaps the hope I had held on to really did have a purpose. Maybe it was the only thing that had brought me through the worst moments of my life.

And then I thought, what if I was just looking at this all wrong? Maybe these men were not so evil at all. As terrifying as they appeared, maybe Bloody Mary was trying to help me, to guide me through the storm, with a team of the undead who couldn't care less how hot or cold Hell was. They were protecting me through the harshest winter I had ever endured. Though Mother and Father had died, perhaps they were all trying to protect me.

I shook my head and bit my tongue, shaking the thought away as soon as it took hold of me. What was I thinking? They had murdered my parents right before my eyes. Something was wrong with me. I couldn't let whatever was holding power over me win. I had become hypnotized, entranced by the reflection in their eyes.

"Go on." Bloody Mary spoke through Marty, who nodded and motioned for me to step into the town. Her tone was light and comforting, but I knew it was all a sham. Though these men had never laid a finger on me, they had imprisoned my reflection in their eyes. "They won't suspect a thing. There is more to your story than you will ever know."

He reached for my necklace, but as his hand made contact with my locket, the metal shimmered and jolted his fingers away with a shock of static electricity.

"Soon, it will be ready, the portal to the other side."

He looked into my eyes, and there, I became lost in the windows to his empty soul. I simply had to comply. I started toward the village. The man carrying logs over his shoulders walked up to me.

"Little girl, are you lost?"

I nodded, but it was Bloody Mary controlling me from afar. "Please…please help me. I am cold."

His forehead creased with concern. "You're sick with fever. Where are your parents?"

"They are frozen."

"Oh, no. Please, do not be afraid. We will warm you up, here at the fire pit." I stepped closer, and as the fire shone into my eyes, the concern in his face turned to fright. I'm sure he could see that emptiness, the infinite reflection of dead starlight, shining through me. "What is this? It can't be. No. Demon. Somebody, help!"

His eyes widened as he stumbled backwards, the logs tumbling off his shoulders. Behind him, villagers started rushing toward him.

"Demon, rid yourself from this poor little girl!"

I smiled as he offered a quiet prayer under his breath. And maybe he was right. Perhaps I was possessed with something like a demon. I was gliding across the ground now, a puppet controlled by the hands of Bloody Mary, the wind nipping my cheeks like a soft winter breeze, the scent of wet dirt and rot filling the air. A mixture of terror and elation churned inside me, a fire blazing through my heart. The adrenaline was so pure that I felt myself lifting from the ground, empowered by the infinite light of the cosmos.

"Give us what we need," I heard myself saying, though when I hear this now in the echoes of my memories, it was never me to begin with. "Pay the price, and we will let your village stand."

"'Atta girl." Marty appeared from the shadows, followed by those other lifeless corpses, who smiled in unison. "Show 'em what you're made of."

Everyone stood there now, watching in awe as I raised my hands into the sky, static ectoplasm bursting from my fingertips. It was then that it hit me—these were those same people I had raised from the dead. The mother, the daughter, standing behind this man, looking at me in terror. I had brought them all back to life, but they could no longer recognize me.

On the trail, I had helped revive those poor, helpless souls with the power of the stars. They had congregated here, at this village, on the threshold of life and death. And now, they stared back at me like a wicked reflection.

I couldn't do this. I felt that same power manifesting in my veins, the starlight that had brought them back, but now, it felt different. Bloody Mary was distorting my mind. She was blurring my memories together with hers, ready to unleash the terror of that dead starlight through my fingertips.

She wanted me to kill them.

She wanted me to destroy them all.

I watched as something like the deadliest lighting hovered over my arms. The ectoplasm was growing now, powered by Marty's locket. I watched the fear grow on the old man's face as he realized he was defenseless against the power of infinity.

But something shook me out of my stupor. It was something about the way I reflected within his eyes, the way the light and the shadows shone through my body, the me that was not there, an empty corpse floating within the window to his soul.

It pulled me out of my trance.

This entire village, a congregation of families and children who had endured one of the harshest winters, was standing there, watching in bloody horror as I rose from the ground, propelled by the light of the forgotten stars.

I had brought them back from the dead, but now, they were afraid of me. I had saved them from eternal darkness, and now, I was about to unleash the dead starlight onto their souls.

I couldn't do this. Whatever Bloody Mary had planned, I couldn't allow her to create this new memory, a memory that was not real to me, to who I was. I could not take the lives of innocent souls.

"No." I turned to Bloody Mary. "No."

"What?" Her voice grew deeper now, merging with the voices of the undead. "What are you saying?"

"I said, no. I will not allow this."

"This was never part of your timeline." Bloody Mary stepped forward, her scar-like smile stretching into the most wicked frown I had ever seen. "If we do not refill your mirror with the reflection of their blood, then none of us will ever make it out alive. Do not be foolish. Do the right thing!"

"And who are you to tell me what is right, when I have seen you take blood before my very eyes?"

"You played with your fate once, Macy. Do it again, and your parents will not only die, again and again, but I will make you watch them, again and again, and you will kill them, again and again, for all of eternity…"

"If all I will become is a memory, then place me back there. I will die a million times before I cause all of these people the same pain you are causing me."

Something within me imploded. It was that feeling of hope within my soul that Father had hinted of. I needed to control it before it overtook me. It was radiating from my heart now, churning within my veins. It was overwhelming. I knew I had a choice. I could either run from it, or run towards it.

The power of infinity sparkled from my fingertips.

The ground lit up in a tidal wave of color as my technicolor shadow hovered in this newfound energy. The memories of the dead and the secrets they contained swirled through my mind. I could feel the weight of the neuroflash hover at the back of my skull. Beneath me, the villagers screamed in horror.

Bloody Mary reached through the mist of ectoplasm that surrounded me. "You are scaring them. Give me your hand."

"If you are going to send me back there, to watch my parents die again, then perhaps I can send myself back there first to rewrite those memories, until I write you out of them, so I can save these people from seeing the likes of you."

"You are ignorant. You should not channel this energy if you cannot understand it. Now that they have all seen these memories, we are at risk. Would you like me to trap you there, in that dead space between the stars, or would you like to break us all out of here?"

"I have already been there, Bloody Mary. I am there now. It is where I have been all along, since my parents died, since I have been floating here in the Interstate." Her eyes widened. "Yes, I know about this place. It's becoming more apparent to me as I remember my memories. But now, I have someone else who can understand. Someone who is waiting for me, there, in the future, ready to hear my story."

Bloody Mary floated into the air, propelled by the ectoplasm dripping from her fingers.

"No one will remember your name," she said.

"I might be forgotten someday, but I will never let you take away the experiences I have shared with the people I love. It is in our blood, isn't it? These memories? This power that controls you?"

She hovered in front of me, studying me. "It is in my blood, but not yours. You will never channel the power of the starlight, and the memories they contain. You will only float there, in that empty, dead place between them, eternally."

Ectoplasm flashed from my fingertips. I brought my hands together and watched as the liquid memories merged into an orb of ethereal light. It was a different type of power that was building inside of me, one that she did not possess. In fact, this very power possessed *her*. In order to make peace with the past and focus on the future, I needed to think clearly, to a memory that awaited me, somewhere beyond the void.

But I couldn't. I felt a mix of rage, regret, and determination. I had been sentenced to relive the worst moments of my life. I had to watch my parents die endlessly, but now, if I was successful, I could save others from the same fate.

I needed to find a way to return to this moment and trap Bloody Mary in order to spare everybody else. It needed to be here, in this place, where I had risen the dead with this same power. It needed to be where the infinite starlight shining in our souls reflected perfectly.

I had to find a way back here, once more, even if it meant I would be risking my own life in the process.

I blasted the orb of ectoplasm into Bloody Mary's locket, and I neuroflashed into the glass, through that dead space between the stars.

CHAPTER TWENTY-SIX

I neuroflashed through the screen and found myself sitting in my apartment.

I took a deep breath and sighed. For a moment I thought I was truly back home. I thought I was safe, neuroflashing years into the future to where I had just been moments ago, when I had first heard of Dianne's passing.

I looked into my computer screen to make sense of my surroundings.

A spirit stared back at me.

I jumped.

"Macy?"

It was my own reflection. I was so disoriented that for a moment I could barely recognize myself. I realized then that it was Halloween 2019, the last spooky celebration of the decade, and I had just neuroflashed to one of the worst nights of my life.

I was about to see Dianne through the window.

Halloween was supposed to be a big day for me. Dianne and I used to spend our Halloweens together all the time. I reached a breaking point that year. I couldn't go one more holiday without seeing her. It had been years of distance, reconnection, more distance, anger, hatred, and then silence.

Sometimes we would say hello over Facebook Messenger, but that was about it.

That year was different, though. No one knew just how difficult the coming months would be. Nobody could have predicted just how much our lives would soon change, readapting to the "new normal" of the lockdown, and maybe that was a blessing in disguise.

The new decade was a new chance at life. At least that's what everyone claimed. For the first time in years, we had a real opportunity to change things. In a few months, we were going to have an entirely clean slate, at least in the eyes of a calendar. We could all start over, because in the year 2020, we would have "perfect vision" and real clarity on the things we wanted to achieve in our lives.

I knew what I wanted.

I wanted Dianne to get better.

I wanted my sister back.

That year, I figured maybe by talking to her, I would help her into a clean and sober decade to come. Even though I had conditioned myself to let go of those feelings, of needing to save her, I shouldn't have messaged her that night when I saw her.

Some Halloweens I saw her through the window, if I was lucky. She didn't know it at the time, but I think she felt my presence. That's probably why she kept coming back, year after year, to know that somebody still cared about her well-being even if they weren't necessarily allowed to show it. She wasn't a ghost to me then. She was somebody living on the edge of life and death, imprisoned in a certain kind of drug-induced limbo, one that would only get worse and worse, and I couldn't keep being the one to pull her out.

She needed to save herself. At least, that's what everyone else told me. I could only do so much.

Every Halloween, I would put out a bowl of candy on a green, plastic folding table, one of its legs bent to the point where if you'd lean on it, it might fold into itself. There wasn't really anybody trick-or-treating in my apartment complex, so I never had a real need to buy a new one. I did, however, invest at least ten bucks or so into buying the best candy I could find, a mix of Reese's pieces, a giant Hershey's bar, and her favorite blue raspberry sour-belts that I had to special order online. I only set the bowl out for her in case she decided to visit, which she almost always did during her drug days.

Oh, yeah. I also put in at least $200 cash at the bottom of the bowl. Not that I had the money. I was barely getting by, but it was the least I could do. And a packet of six spooky, silly pairs of socks with ghosts and ghouls on them. It was a mini care package. I couldn't help myself. I was probably giving her mixed signals. I'd told her she could no longer ask me for money. That was probably one of the hardest moments of my life. She probably still would have come just for the candy, but since she wasn't in the right state of mind, I figured another incentive couldn't hurt. Maybe it was more for me than it was for her.

I saw her through the window, then, back in the past, now.

At first, through the broken, gray blinds of my apartment, she was a mere silhouette blending in with the costumed creatures wandering the streets beyond. Before she even approached, I kind of already knew she was coming. It was weird. It happened every year, too. Not that I was actually psychic or anything. I had a feeling it was the supernatural bond that only siblings share.

And then she emerged out of the darkness.

My stomach dropped.

She looked awful. Truly. She looked terrible. And it made me feel awful to see her like that. The harsh, automatic light above my apartment shone on her, casting a spotlight on her pale, lifeless skin. She looked into the light and froze. It was almost as if she had forgotten where she was, and maybe she had. Maybe she was just on autopilot at that point.

I didn't want to know what drugs she was on. I couldn't fathom what was pumping through her veins. She looked like she was wearing a costume, even though she was just wearing her street clothes. Her skin was barely hanging on to her bones. Her eyes were empty, lost, searching for some reason to keep walking. Her staggered breathing sent shivers down my spine.

She reached into the bowl. Torn, ragged bits of open cysts hung from her hand, blood quietly sprinkling the table as she searched for the money, almost as though she was panning for gold. She was barely moving but couldn't stop moving, tweaking in the smallest ways, as though she was caught in some invisible current, moving slowly with the tide until it consumed her.

I couldn't help it. I had to make myself known. I hadn't texted her in about eight months so I though that was a good start. I didn't want to put her on the spot. I didn't want to scare her away like I had before. So I just texted her hello.

I saw her jump slightly as her phone chimed and vibrated in her pocket. She pulled it out and stared at it. It was a wonder that it was even working at all. Her head lolled slightly, nodding, as she opened the message. She texted me back, but her response was so nonsensical that even autocorrect couldn't find the meaning of her words.

So, I did the only thing I could think of.

I opened the door.

"Dianne." I was about to step outside but instead remained in the doorway. I didn't want to overwhelm her. Chills ran down my spine as I stood face to face with a ghost. "Hi."

"Hey." She looked up and smiled, a mix of delight and despair. Her words was slurred, soft. She coughed. "Erica."

"Happy Halloween." I had never felt so hopeful and hopeless at the same time. She was already too far gone, but she also wasn't. I had to use my words carefully, contain the nervousness in my voice. "I picked out your favorite candy this year. Remember those sour-belts?" She nodded. "You were obsessed. We'd get so sugar high. Didn't we?"

"Hell yeah."

"I miss that. We had so much fun together."

"It's just candy." She hesitated and winced, as though disgusted by the memories she possessed. She reached into the bowl of candy and pulled out the stack of cash. "We're not kids anymore, Erica."

"No, we're not." I stepped out of the doorframe into the cold night. It looked like she hadn't showered in months. "But I love you just the same."

She looked up. "You do?"

"Yes. Very much."

We stood there for a moment, studying each other. I studied my reflection in her eyes. Somewhere, deep below, Bloody Mary was waiting to resurface. Normally, Dianne looked through me, unaware that her younger sister was trying to guide her toward happiness, but that night, and now, it seemed as though she actually recognized who I was. Oftentimes, it appeared she just lived in perpetual memories, lost in a blur of time and a haze of hyper-focused awareness. But for a moment, I swore I saw a flicker of light in her eyes, of understanding, of acknowledgement, of hope.

Tonight, I would not let her memories, or Bloody Mary, possess her.

"Yeah, of course," I said. "I love you a lot, actually."

She held up the money, studying it. "That's nice of you."

"I know you could use it."

"What did you say?" She cocked her head. "Yes, I can. I know we haven't talked in a while, Erica. But I dream about you, and even in my dreams you won't talk to me."

"I'm sorry. Sometimes I don't know what to say."

"No, really. I message you and message you and you leave me on *read*. What did I do to you? You think I'm a tweaker?"

"No."

"Then why would I need money? Because I do. But how would you know?"

"Because you're my sister. Remember, we know everything about each other."

"I remember you, I think." She laughed and then coughed again. "What was your name again?"

"Erica." My heart sank. "I'm Erica, Dianne. I'm your sister. You were my best friend for years."

"That sounds lovely. We're not kids anymore, are we? Because there's sugar rushes, but then there's…this."

She began to pull something out of her purse.

"No, Dianne. Stop."

"Stop what?"

"Just come inside."

"Why would I wanna do that? More people waiting for me inside again? You gonna have one of those meetings?"

"No. It's cold out. Come inside."

"Not gonna fall for your interventions again." She pulled a needle out of her purse. "Besides, I'm never cold anymore, not with this."

"Dianne, what is that?"

"Wouldn't you like to know? They say it's like *yaba* but sweeter. Here, give me your arm."

"No."

"You never text me back. I don't want that anymore."

"Me neither."

"Then just text me," Dianne snapped.

"I can't."

"Why not?"

"Not when you're like this."

"Like what?" She stepped forward slowly, her eyes locked on my shoulders. Bloody Mary was dancing within her eyes, directing Dianne towards my body. "Here, give me your arm. It'll be real quick and easy."

"Dianne."

"Yeah?"

"Stop."

"It'll just be a light poke." She looked at the needle in her hand. Her eyes widened as she recognized what she was doing. There was a battle there, between heaven and hell, within her eyes. She quickly stashed the needle away. "Oh, no. I'm sorry. I'm so sorry."

"It's okay."

"I would never hurt you. Never."

Her purse slipped out of her grasp. She fumbled for it, sticking thumbprints of blood on the handle. I was going to try to hug her, to remind her of what it meant to be human, to feel the warmth of another soul close to hers, but she stepped away.

"You're bleeding," I said.

"I'm fine."

"Let me get you a band-aid."

She blinked. "I'm fine, really. I can just get some from the gas station. They never notice what's missing."

"Dianne. Listen to me. You need help."

"Who are you again?"

"You need *help* help."

"Shut up. You don't even know me." She shook her head and placed her hands on her hips. It was almost comical, like a cartoon character shaking their head in relief after just dodging a falling anvil. "You jerk. You can't tell me what to do. We're not kids anymore."

A look of terror fell across Dianne's face as she momentarily broke through her high, now, in the present, in the past. But there, dancing deliriously in her eyes, was Bloody Mary, ready to break through.

I took a deep breath and focused on that space between the stars. I needed to conquer the memories of my past in order to fully channel the power of the dead starlight above. I needed to shine from within. I would face Bloody Mary soon. I felt it in my blood, and this time, I would not let her win.

"Erica, what's happening to me?" It was Dianne, but not from this memory. She was somewhere else, on the other side of Bloody Mary's mirror, somewhere far into the afterlife. "Who have I become?"

"It's okay. We'll get you safe. We'll get you clean. Just listen to my voice. You're not yourself. But we can change that. I can help you remember who you are."

"There's something else in me. It's like pure evil, in my blood. There are demons in my brain. I'm trapped here, Erica. Please, save me."

I reached out to Dianne to pull her through, but my hand fell through her grasp, just as it had before.

Dianne blinked.

Blood fell from her eyes.

"Dianne!"

"Erica!"

Bloody Mary's ectoplasm burst through Dianne's eyes like termites drilling through a screen door. Her head squished through and her body stretched out beneath her, but she couldn't break free from Dianne's gaze.

"I know you've been there for a long time, Bloody Mary. I've seen it myself, when I saw my life flash before my eyes. But now, you must let my sister go."

I felt the ectoplasm sparkling in my veins. I was prepared to manifest the infinite memories of the cosmos through my fingertips.

"I would like that as well, Erica. Soon, I will stand before you, and I will no longer be speaking to you through this side of the mirror. But before that happens, we must realize where you had gone wrong. You were so close to saving her." She opened Dianne's purse and emptied its contents into the bowl of candy. "You knew what she had here. She even showed you. And you certainly knew she could have been days away from dying. Why didn't you just take her inside and make her get help? What stopped you?"

"I did! I tried everything! I tried and nothing worked!"

"No, that's not it. You didn't succeed because you were scared. You were like a deer frozen in the headlights. You were shocked, seeing her like this, that's it. Here she was, ready to be saved, but you weren't strong enough. You weren't there for her when she needed you the most."

Bloody Mary took the needle out of the candy bowl and raised it to her arms.

"You're wrong. I was there for her then, and I'm here for her now, as I always have been."

Ectoplasm burst out of my fingertips and pierced through the syringe. It broke and the liquid within splashed across the Dianne's face.

Dianne clasped her hands to her eyes and screamed.

"Dianne," I said, reaching out to her again. "I didn't mean to—"

"Why'd you do that, Erica? Why did you leave me like this? Why did you kill me?"

Bursts of light flashed across the apartment complex as crimson memories blasted from Bloody Mary's hands. They barreled through my chest and sent me crashing through the doorframe.

Stars filled my vision as my head collided into the tile walkway leading to the living room. I gasped for air. I pushed myself up as the ghosts of my past hovered through my doorway.

I reached to the back of my skull. When I pulled my hand back, my fingertips were covered with blood.

Bloody Mary laughed. "That's right, Erica. You are quickly merging into your former self. You weren't strong back then, so you will die here, now, where no one will remember you."

I reached for purchase as Bloody Mary hovered over me, my dead sister's frail body floating inches from my face. The sharp scents of death and decay trailed in the air. A mist of crimson ectoplasm surrounded me.

"I will die here, right now, if that means Dianne will be free to live again, somewhere in the afterlife."

"That doesn't make sense, Erica. Why does it matter now that she's dead?"

"Because I have seen my life flash before my eyes, and I know what it is like, without her in it." I stood. Blood fell from my fingertips and merged with the ectoplasm. "But I also know what it is like, with her in my life. I can see you there, through my sister's eyes, waiting to break free. But as I stand before you, I am no longer afraid. I can feel the power of those dead memories that have haunted you shining in my blood. And it does not scare me."

"Liar." Bloody Mary frowned. I pushed myself away from her and stood, but the weight of the ectoplasm pulled me back towards her. "Liar. You see nothing."

"I see it all clearly now. I have found the trail to the other side of your mirror, Bloody Mary, and it's in your eyes, as it has been all along."

Chills ran down my spine as I stood face to face with Bloody Mary. There, in my sister's eyes, through Bloody Mary's veil of crimson ectoplasm, I saw someone else reflecting within.

I had become a stranger to myself, back then, when I was here, once before, staring into my sister's eyes. I had not been able to recognize the person standing before me, and I couldn't remember who was staring back within. We had both been living in fear, afraid of who we had become.

But now, as I stood here again, in this moment, now, I had the power to become someone else. I could save Dianne, even if it meant I would be trapped there, on the other side of Bloody Mary's mirror, forever.

The colors of the universe shifted through me as I saw myself radiating in Bloody Mary's eyes.

It was happening.

I was becoming her reflection.

Our memories merged together as I neuroflashed through the mirror of her eyes into the other side beyond.

CHAPTER TWENTY-SEVEN

Remember, Erica?

When we went on a field trip to pan for gold?

I was thinking about it tonight because I just saw an ad for that game come up on my timeline. Tour's been fun. Got wasted the other night. The ad was a picture of a T-shirt with a green, pixelated wagon, and underneath, there was some quote about it from the game, talking about dying from something terrible. I clicked on it, only for a sec, 'cuz it caught my eye. And then it started popping up on every. Single. Platform.

Literally. Instagram. Twitter. Even Tik Tok. The same freaking ad. I swear, sometimes the algorithm sees all. Haha. Maybe I've been playing too many free games online or something. I think it's the same companies, or the companies merged by now, but somehow it popped up. You gotta fill up your time with something, I suppose. I have no shame whatsoever. No shame. I'll keep growing my digital farm until the day I die.

You were in the third grade, and Mom was supposed to be one of your class's chaperones, but she couldn't make it, so I went in her place instead, mainly just to skip class, not gonna lie, *lol*. But I also went because I loved spending time with you. I really did. Even though I'd gone on that same exact field trip before, it was nice to re-experience it through your eyes. You were always so curious. It was contagious.

You were so worried about the written report you had to turn in at the end of the day. If I wasn't there, you probably would have missed out on some of the fun. You thought you had so much more responsibility then, so much to prove, having just crossed the threshold from second grade to third. Maybe you were doing it to impress me, to show me how diligent you always were. You were acting kind of different, like you were sad about something, but I didn't know what. It's funny how time works that way. I was just two years older than you, but maybe you even thought I was an adult. I'm almost thirty now. Isn't that weird? Really, really weird?

We rode the bus together to Old Town, San Diego, and we were playing thumb war, which, surprisingly, you were pretty dang good at. I brought up Bloody Mary, but you just shook your head. You didn't want to even hear her name. You looked like you went somewhere else in your head for a moment. I mentioned how no one knew where Bloody Mary came from and they just had theories about a queen who bathed in blood. You remained silent. You had just snuck a few bites of a cookie from your epic, sparkly Pokemon lunch bag, because I remember you having crumbs on your thumb. I asked you where you kept your secret stash, and you laughed so loud that Mrs. Garmain looked back. I think you even yelled *"duuuuuck"* and we hid there for a moment, until you sidled over the cushion, waving to the adults in the front, who waved happily back. And then you hooked me up with the good stuff. We were feeling the sugar rush for sure.

I think it must have been on a Friday or something, because everyone had really good vibes all around. You could tell there was a certain type of excitement in the air, even with the parents and the teachers. It was like Halloween energy, because we were going somewhere different to become something else. We were traveling between two worlds—the past and the future, happily willing to suspend our disbelief to forget the present. Not that we weren't in the moment, though. It was a new moment, floating between two realms.

We had become timeless, then.

"Do you think it was like this?" You were staring out the window, eyes full of curiosity and wonder. You placed your hand up against the glass, almost reaching through it, and when you pulled your hand off, it was still there, floating in the sky.

"Do you think *what* was like *what* now?"

"Back in the olden days. You know, when they were traveling on the trail to California. Do you think it was like this, on the other side? That it was waiting for them all along?"

"What was waiting for them? Gold?"

"No. This feeling. Like everything was worth it."

I thought for a moment.

I looked through the window, to Old Town beyond, but you were stuck there still, your handprint fading on the window, the world moving through your transparent fingertips.

-Dianne

CHAPTER TWENTY-EIGHT

After I went back into the locket, I found myself suspended in time, neuroflashing to the future, to the past, over and over again.

I flashed to a place where I was used as bait, a lone wanderer taking advantage of lost families. I cried for help, and they gave me food, and then Marty and his men were about to kill them all. I don't want to speak about this, Erica. But before Marty and his men could kill them all, I found a way to neuroflash back through the locket, to the very moment my parents died, to the lonesome wandering of that lonely year, to the moment I neuroflashed again and again and again to the day my parents were killed.

But I still could not find my way back to that village, to that sanctuary of the souls I had helped save. Bloody Mary knew the destination I had in mind. I was caught in a loop, Erica. I couldn't break out of it, not until I heard you shout into your very own void. Perhaps I had flashed a million times to these moments, where I was about to help these men kill them all, but I never did, because of you.

But something has changed.

I can't hear your voice.

I know you're there, on the other side, but I can't hear you anymore.

Where are you, Erica?

I was somewhere in the ever-expanding darkness. Though my hands were not tied, I sat alone in the back of Bloody Mary's wagon, imprisoned by the wild snow around me. If I were with Mother and Father, we would have celebrated our progress toward our goal, more than halfway to experiencing a rush of happiness during that Gold Rush. But as I sat in the back of the wagon, desperately planning my moment of escape, I wished we had never left for California in the first place.

Why would we have ever taken this journey if we knew what it would cost? Would we have descended into the frozen terrors beyond if we had known the price we would pay? I couldn't contemplate the reasons why anyone would have traveled this far, all for the prospect of becoming a Prospect, a prisoner to the panning and panting as we would search for even a small glimmer of gold.

Though my story was still being written, and still is, in a sense, Mother's and Father's had been cut short, all because they wanted to provide me with a better life. They had sacrificed everything, all for me. It seemed pointless, then.

In that moment, both now and back then, I longed to be beside Mother again. I longed to hear Father's laugh, his gentle humming, even if we were inevitably progressing into the eye of an unseen storm. I longed to hear Bessie's gentle neighing, her fierce resilience in the arctic tundra. But none of those things remained, and if they did, they were locked within the locket, in the realm of my memories that I would soon relive, if I did not comply to Bloody Mary's demands.

Now, I had to face it alone. I had to make my own decisions. I had to trust my intuition. Using only the stars and the power they provided through my locket as my guide, I had to trust that this would work out. And it wasn't until you came along that I became aware of this vicious cycle, aware that maybe I could hold on to hope, just a little longer.

At last, the wagon came to a halt. Bloody Mary and the other men told me to get out and do as they said, and if I didn't, they would flash me back to the past. I followed them through the shadows to a series of boulders.

I knew I had already lived this moment before I saw it play out. My mind couldn't wrap around the inherent cosmic structures that were soon to be revealed. I was re-experiencing the very moment my parents had died, but from a different vantage point.

In the distance, I heard Father humming that gentle tune, Bessie neighing in harmony.

I almost cried out. He had meant for me to hear this. Father knew I would be here, listening to his song through the valleys from afar. Though there are many unknowns in this universe, Erica, at that moment I knew Father understood the power of infinity. He had tried expressing this to me. He knew that the song of his heart would be heard, even if he was no longer living. His spirit was singing to me from beyond the grave.

"Bloody Mary leaned over to the right side of the boulder, inspecting the wagon.

"Don't you dare say a peep," she said.

"Don't worry," I replied, picking up a rock and hiding it between my hands. "I won't say a single word."

And I didn't. I'm not one to break my promises, Erica, even to those evil men, unless I was telling a white lie, of course, which I rarely did. But right then, as my parents' wagon approached about fifty feet away, ready to pass through to the threshold of life and death, I mustered up the last strength I possessed.

I propelled the dead starlight from my fingertips into the air with the last bit of ectoplasm that my spirit contained. I launched the same rock that had hit our wagon's front wheel memories ago. I had become something like a reflection within a reflection of my former self, and in that moment, I was my own guardian angel, watching over us, all along. A hidden place in my heart allowed this, a place of memories both known and unknown, the intuitive force guiding me through the unknown.

And in that moment, I risked everything.

"Girl!" Bloody Mary started toward me, ready to flash me back into her own locket, but as the other men ran into the snow, she had no choice but to keep up. If they didn't act at that very moment, then my parents perhaps never would have died.

Now was my chance.

I was right there, in that same spot where the constellations had shone onto me and where Bloody Mary's voice had spoken to me before. I reflected the sky through the looking glass. I placed my hand on my locket, and the ectoplasm swirled through my body again, and then, in the midst of the flash, I heard you cry out to the void, and I went there, to that place in the Interstate, where I first spoke to you.

But as soon as I did, Bloody Mary listened, and I flashed back through to the other side again, back into my wagon, where I watched them die, again and again, endlessly, for years that stretched into eternities.

Sometimes, I am afraid there's no way out, Erica.

Father spoke of hope. But I am not sure there is any point to holding onto hope any longer. He told me that I was a gift, and a weapon. Maybe I am neither of those things, Erica. I am just a lost soul floating between the dead space between the stars.

But if I keep trying, I can neuroflash back to that village, to that safe place I have built through these memories. It is the sanctuary that has been waiting for me at the other end of this trail.

They are waiting for me to return, those lost spirits I had brought back to life. And so are you. But I am trapped here, Erica. Please, help me.

Perhaps there is nothing on the other end of this trail at all.

Tell me, Erica, what do you see?

CHAPTER TWENTY-NINE

DIANNE

lease.

Please answer.

I love you.

Very very much!!!!!!!!!

I love you, Er-Bear.

You are my person.

Please forgive me.

I dropped the phone as the last text went through.

My hands were shaking.

I was sinking.

Something in the chemicals didn't quite mix right.

I took too much.

It was finally happening.

What you told me never would.

You were there, always, Erica, and then you weren't. But you were there, on the other side, because I had wished upon a star for it.

That's what we were.

We were two stars, then, two mirrors infinitely reflecting the same source of light.

But now, Erica, I am fading.

CHAPTER THIRTY

I neuroflashed through the closet mirror of my childhood home and found myself sitting awake on the carpet in my bedroom, trying to battle insomnia. I wanted to play computer games because I couldn't sleep and it was winter break, but I didn't want Mom and Dad to get annoyed that I was up late. My mind spun, trying to make sense of the visions I had seen when I saw my life flash before my eyes. A moment ago, in my head, I was there, in the future. But there I was, now, in the past.

I needed a distraction. So I played the games in my head. *Rollercoaster Tycoon*, *The Sims*, *The Oregon Trail*. "The works," Dad would say, like the bagels he used to get at Pete's Coffee. "All the good stuff," Dianne called it. We couldn't afford much but we had built our collection over the years and we'd play for so long that when I would blink, the screen would still be there, a faint, blue outline that closed itself around me.

Some nights, when I couldn't fall asleep, when Bloody Mary's crimson shadows started pulling me into the full-sized mirror on my closet door, I would play the games in my head. I wasn't allowed to stay up past nine, maybe ten at the max, so I had to do something to cure the fact that I couldn't get the heck to sleep.

I did everything I could to not think of the near future, moments ago, when Dianne would die. I didn't know that insomnia was a symptom of anxiety. I was just doing anything I could to keep my mind off things, off the shadows, off the infinite trail of blood I had seen in the mirror. I couldn't keep thinking about the things I'd seen when my life flashed before my eyes, before I even had a chance to experience them. So, I tried to go to that happy place in my head when I became sad.

Dianne and I shared a bunk bed, and she was snoring above me, probably dreaming of Pokemon or something, when I saw the world from a third-person point of view.

I was in a game. There, in the future, I was living in my own version of the simulations I had played. I was living in the pandemic, alone, in my apartment. In order to win, all I had to do was wait. What was on the other side of this trail?

I could see everything. All of the video games were right within reach. I could see myself playing them, and in my head, I was able to pull up any video game I wanted. I imagined myself there, in rollercoaster land, an entire theme park made out of bathrooms, because it was simply funny to do. I would delete the pathways to the entrances and exits to watch them get confused. These people didn't know why, but now, they were stuck in the bathrooms forever.

And then I saw myself playing *The Sims*, where I transformed into a middle-aged painter dude in a virtual neighborhood, trying to level up my skills to get a promotion to make fake money to find a fake spouse to make a fake family with, until I fake died and wanted to start a new life altogether. It seemed so simple, to go from point A to point Z, leveling up until you beat the game and started over again.

And then I pictured myself in that other video game. The one I was living in, now. A game of life, a game of death. I was on an endless trail traveling through the darkness.

Something within my mind shifted.

Even in my head, I became out of body, almost as though I was floating, watching myself staring at myself in the screen playing the game.

I was becoming an infinite reflection. Perhaps I had been trapped there, in that dead place, always.

The other games weren't like this one.

They were fun. They were silly. You could create a rollercoaster and then you could hire a park entertainer to become a panda to make families giggle with joy. You could buy balloons and then pop them before they reached the sky. You could name your character Mister Cool Guy and meet fake people and buy cool virtual objects, like a new TV or a stainless steel, state-of-the-art microwave or shower. You could buy pizza and get a job and then buy more pizza with the money you made. After you leveled up, you could win.

But this one was different.

In the game I was living in now, all I had to do was survive.

It became real to me, then, right in that very moment.

I was no longer staring through a screen but through a one-way mirror, watching as these characters died, suffering endlessly. I could only sit there, watching as they traveled through the trail, again and again. I tried to tell them that it was just a game, but they couldn't hear me. I tried turning off the computer in my head, but it wouldn't unplug.

The screen dissolved, and I floated somewhere, in that space between the stars.

The dead starlight reached for me. Dianne was there, too. I heard her breathing at the other end. I called to her, but she couldn't hear me. I had become motionless.

The darkness had a certain shape to it, almost cylindrical, as though a narrow tunnel was infinitely unspooling itself. Something was waiting for me, then and now, as I relived these moments, in the shadows, beneath that dead starlight.

I was trapped in that place, watching the world from above. I was sinking further into the sky.

The game restarted, again and again, in my head. It was no longer a game. It was a trail. I was trapped in the sky, reaching for anything to hold on to as the universe folded into itself.

I had seen Bloody Mary then, and I would see her soon, now.

I knew exactly where I was, where I had been trapped all along.

I was in that dead space between the stars, where memories die.

CHAPTER THIRTY-ONE

MACY

I fell out of the locket, having just seen my parents die, my heart breaking, my mind reeling with shock, my spirit weak and frail. If Father told me to hold on to hope, even for a little longer, then I needed to endure whatever waited for me in the shadows beyond. I needed to remember Father's courage to withstand the terrors waiting for me, no matter how difficult they might be.

As the ectoplasm shimmered and faded around me, I found myself standing in the same village where I'd encountered the souls I had raised from the dead.

Somehow, with your help, Erica, I had found my way back to this memory. But now, I would have to rewrite it before my very eyes.

You had listened to my cry for help, years in the future, and now, I believe we will both face Bloody Mary.

She was hiding, lurking in the shadows. Now was my chance to remind these villagers that I was not the same spirit who had killed them all.

They were all watching me, speechless. The villagers were holding pitchforks now, staring at me, studying me, venom swirling through their eyes. Perhaps Bloody Mary had entranced them, too.

The sharp scent of smoke trailed through the air as they stepped closer, waving their lanterns and torches in the sky, illuminating me.

"Is it her?" It was the old man who had been carrying logs. The mother and daughter I had raised from the dead stood behind them, holding piles of splintered wood.

Even though I had grown used to the cold, shivers ran up and down my spine.

"It is she." Bloody Mary spoke from behind me, enunciating as though she were a nobleperson. She was hiding within Marty's eyes, hovering within. She had already infiltrated this moment before I could rewrite it. She had transcended my memories and had placed herself here, in the future that had never been.

"I am nothing more than a memory. But this man who stands before you hasn't just stared death in the face. He is death."

"What riddles plague your tongue?" Bloody Mary laughed. "You will no longer have a reason to fear the dark, everyone, for this demon will die."

"That is not true. I will prove it to you." I tried conjuring the power of the starlight within my veins, but something else eclipsed them. "You must believe me. I cannot die, because I have been exiled here, by you, Bloody Mary, to relive the worst moments of my life. But in this endless eternity, it is I who has brought you all back to life! I have held onto hope, with the help of my friend, and now you have experienced hope, too. Have you all forgotten?"

"Brought us back to life?" Bloody Mary said. "There is only one spirit who can transcend death. Do not speak blasphemous words."

The villagers raised their pitchforks high into the air. I could almost hear the metal slashing the sky in half.

"Please," I screamed. "It's her, there, in his eyes. You might not understand but I am lost somewhere in time, trapped in these memories."

"Do not let the Devil's tongue whisper lies unto our ears," the old man said, throwing the logs behind his shoulders. "You cannot fool us, demon. Everyone, quickly, gather round the village square while we still have the chance. Now!"

They came toward me, then. The very souls I had raised from the dead, the families, the children, the parents I had gifted a second chance of life, who had been slaughtered by Bloody Mary and the undead men she stood beside, were now rushing toward me, pitchforks locking me in place, flames hovering inches above my face.

I tried to move but the fire danced around my forehead. I opened my locket and saw the picture of Father and Mother staring back, frozen in time. I stared deeply into the mirror, wishing upon a star that all of the stars in the universe would alight through the looking glass and cast a fire through my veins, empowering me with ectoplasm to guide me through this moment.

But I saw nothing.

Only an endless void.

Even my own reflection was gone.

"Please. Let me go."

They bound my hands with a frayed rope. It burnt as it rubbed against my wrists. They pushed me to the village square, slowly, steadily, marching in unison as though in a spiritual procession. I screamed to the universe, to my parents, to Bloody Mary herself, until they led me to where they had just finished securing the logs they had thrown over their shoulders underneath a wooden plank.

In the center was a wooden stake.

"No." They dragged me onto the plank. "Please." I heard myself saying these words, but they seemed to come from somewhere else.

In the distance, Bloody Mary's laughter echoed as they bound my hands to the stake. Beneath me, the logs settled into place.

My heartbeat rattled through my bones, whispering through every inch of my skin, trailing through my body like a gust of wind rustling through the eaves of an abandoned house. I was shaking in place, bound by the rope they had tied me with.

Would this be the last memory I would possess?

By dying, would that allow my parents to live? Would I become a memory, long forgotten, as though I had never existed? My mind swirled with delirious words, bits of sentences pulsing through my brain like the birth of the stars, sparking life and death in one Big Bang, the universe collapsing within itself, into myself.

I didn't want to die, Erica.

Nobody does.

But maybe I had to.

I had channeled the starlight, and I had brought the dead back to life. But they no longer knew who I was. I was floating there, now, in that dead space between the stars, and I could not feel them shine within me. Perhaps I needed to die, here in these eternal flames, to pull myself out of these memories, to help them remember, too.

The old man walked up to the pile of wood and stood beside Bloody Mary. He turned to the villagers. "You folks won't have no reason to worry no more, not with this demon tied right here. What should we do, then?"

"Kill her!"

"Burn her!"

"Let the flames repent her wicked soul, banishing her to the depths of hell!"

They roared, their voices echoing throughout the farthest reaches of the Oregon Trail. They raised their pitchforks and their torches, the flames elongating, slithering into the night, dancing like serpent tongues.

"But wait. We first must let her speak." It was the mother whom I had saved on the trail. Perhaps she was starting to remember me. "Her mortal soul may still be trapped within."

"Yes, let her speak." It was Bloody Mary now, watching me through the fire. "Demon, why have you done this? Why did you tamper with fate?"

I almost laughed. They say when you are about to die, you can become hysterical, as though everything is illuminated and the world wobbles and you are there, deliriously, contemplating what resides on the other side. It was almost comical, Erica, because I was staring right at the very men who had killed my parents a million times over.

But I couldn't tell them that. No one would believe me. I took a deep breath, inhaling the smoke trailing from their torches. I coughed and cleared my throat.

"I am not a demon, but an angel." At this, Bloody Mary winced. But I didn't back down. I projected through the flames surrounding me. "I have traveled through the universe to bring light to those who have lost their way on the trail of our lives."

"If you are an angel," Bloody Mary said, "then prove it."

My stomach twirled as Bloody Mary's reflections wheeled in their haunted wagon to the village square. From the back, they dragged something out.

Mother and Father.

Their lifeless bodies, dragged by the dead through the snow.

My heart dropped. The weight of the universe collapsed into my chest. I stood there, my hands bound, helpless, as they brought their bodies to the foot of the wooden plank.

"If you are who you say you are," Bloody Mary said, "then bring these fallen souls who we have found dead on the Oregon Trail back to life."

I couldn't look at them.

I couldn't stand it.

I could hear them dying, in those memories that I had been forced to relive. The moment of their deaths kept flashing before my eyes, but to see them lying there, lifeless, two carcasses for the vultures, I could not stand it.

So, I turned away, squeezing my eyes shut.

"Ah…see? She cannot look at these poor, innocent souls, because she is not who she says she is. She herself has destroyed them. You have one last chance, girl. Show us the light that you claim to contain. If you are who you say you are, then show us the power that rests in your soul."

I had no words. I tried to open my mouth to speak, but the delirium started kicking in. I had lost the life force that had brought back those souls to life.

The fire crackled slowly, like a mere bonfire we had created to feed ourselves along the way to the land of gold. And if I pretended that's what it was, and that Dad was just sleeping, and soon he would cook us our dinner, then it wasn't so bad. But one by one, the villagers lowered their torches, and the logs lit up, and the end of the wooden plank started catching fire, and my life flashed endlessly before my eyes.

"Good, it is done, then." Bloody Mary held up her necklace and opened up her locket. "Go on. Look, look deeply into the mirror. Watch as the flames creep up, surrounding you, ensnaring you. Allow it to cleanse your wicked soul. Let the blood you have stolen from this earth spill forth from your veins, showering you in a baptismal reawakening."

I did not want to know what was on the other side of that mirror. It reflected the flames and the tears spilling from my eyes as I cried out to the universe, through the void, crying to you, Erica, for an end to this madness, for someone, anyone to hear, to pull me out of this vicious cycle of my memories.

"If you are who you say you are," Bloody Mary said, "then bring yourself back to life."

But I couldn't.

I was dying.

I watched as blood covered my body.

And deep within Bloody Mary's mirror, I saw myself transform in front of my very eyes. The reflection of my locket was infinitely reflecting within hers. And in those reflections of reflections, Macy Abigayle was no longer staring back.

The reflection of her was covered in blood. And then it raised its hands, the ectoplasm surging through its fingertips, preparing to unleash the power of infinite dead starlight onto anyone who called her name.

I had evolved into the very thing we have been running from.

She sent me to the other side of the universe, where memories go to die, in her place.

Maybe I had been her all along.

I promise you, Erica. I swear on my parents' lifeless bodies that I did not remember what I became back then, until this very moment, when I neuroflashed through those infinite portals of memories to the other side, beyond, to you.

CHAPTER THIRTY-TWO

"*Macy, you are not her. Just hold on a little longer. I have heard your story and I am here for you, right now, in this very moment. You need to hold onto hope. I can't see you, but I can feel you, and I know that you are not the monster you think you became.*"

~ ~ ~

I was floating through the Interstate, on the trail to Bloody Mary's mirror, further into that dead space between the stars.

It was an endless, glassy horizon that stretched out infinitely around me. There were no memories here. I could barely remember how I had gotten here.

Dianne.

The ectoplasm around my body sparkled. Though I was nowhere, my heart was my home, and in it were the memories I had been trying so desperately to run away from. It guided me through this place, through the terrors of nothingness.

I became transparent as the light of the universe trailed through my veins.

I was growing stronger. Memories cycled through my mind in one giant blur of a timeline, like a social media profile, which reflected into me. It kept me floating here, sustained in the in-between, falling endlessly into myself.

I was stuck within the mirror, desperate to find a way out.

"Macy. Are you okay? Can you hear me?"

"I am sorry, Erica." Macy's voice was a mere whisper, coated in infinite reverb, as though she were calling to me from the end of some ancient moratorium leagues below the sea. "I did not mean to lie to you. I have never comprehended the sheer power of infinity until I saw my reflection merge into hers. I'm about to neuroflash back again to the day my parents died. And then I will become her, again. I will fall into Bloody Mary's eyes and I will forget myself. I can't do this again."

"I'll find a way, Macy. Just don't stop talking." A sudden silence followed. Had I lost her? "You aren't her, I promise. You are you and do not think for a second otherwise. I'll find a way to pull us out. Please, I need to hear your voice to know where you are. Please, say something." I spoke desperately.

"I'm stuck here, aren't I? I thought this would be simple. I thought that by reaching out to you, we'd both feel a little better, because our timelines crossed in such a way that the stars needed to align to make that happen. My memories are blurring with hers, because I am her. I am her true reflection, and now, you are risking your own identity to become hers."

"I don't want to see you suffer any longer. It's not your fault. We'll find a way out. The only way *is* out. I'm going there now. I will get you both out, you and Dianne. I have seen it in Bloody Mary's eyes, in your eyes, in Dianne's eyes. Even if it takes an eternity, we will do this."

"I have always been stuck there, in the past, until you came along, just as you were stuck, then, when you first looked into the mirror and saw what I became. A mirror is a strange thing, Erica. Sometimes, when you look so long into it, you start seeing someone else. A ghost."

"No. Macy, stop."

"But I wouldn't have known what to do if you didn't shout your wish into your profile's timeline. Because when your heart cries out to the universe, you aren't just shouting into an empty void. Time works differently in the universe. The stars we see today are not the same stars that have existed. Their light takes light-years for us to see, and by the time we see them, they might already be gone, just like I am, now. I am not who you think I am."

"You're still here with me, and I won't let you go. Macy Abigayle, you did not die a thousand times to let Bloody Mary win."

In the distance, the sky shook.

"Did you hear that, Erica? It's too late. Bloody Mary knows you have found the trail to the other side of her mirror. She can feel you neuroflashing through her eyes."

My mind was racing, trying to find a way out of this. A way to save us both. "Macy, I saw her once, but I wasn't strong enough back then to fight her. Because, back then, I didn't know how precious life was. When my life flashed before my eyes, I didn't understand it. If I need to pay a price to have lived these memories, then I will be ready, now."

"What do you mean?" Macy's voice grew louder, and the ectoplasm around my body grew in intensity. "Hurry, Erica. I can feel my neuroflash activating. Soon, I will be her again. I will flash to the times I was dying, infinitely reflecting into the mirror, reborn, dead, evolving, like those very men who killed my parents."

"How long have I been trapped here, Macy? How long have I stared into your eyes, becoming her reflection? When will I break through to the other end of your mirror?"

I stared deeply into her eyes.

"You are there now, Erica. Do you remember?"

CHAPTER THIRTY-THREE

ERICA

The weight of my memories collapsed into my chest as I neuroflashed through Macy's eyes.

"Dianne was just with me, Macy. She was right here, looking into the same mirror, wasn't she?" We had just been ten and now I was twenty-eight and I was falling into the darkness and it was grabbing hold of me. "Oh god oh god please help me."

I didn't want to see Dianne again, living, knowing she would die, that the stars would eat her up.

My memories stretched out before me, growing larger, exponentially reflecting upon themselves, pulling in every direction until they became the horizon. The shadows were like dead starlight, shifting through the air as the cosmos dripped through the void. The light I had come to know was gone.

But I could still hear her voice.

"We're not kids anymore, Erica," Dianne was saying, somewhere at the other end of the universe, the mirror, where we had just been.

I've been trapped here for a while, Macy, haven't I?

And then, just as I thought I had found a way out, you were there, too. At the end of the ocean of glass, you stood there, Macy, raising your locket into the sky. You called out to me, your voice a mere whisper, and you told me to run,

run while you still can, because you were changing, and there was nothing you could do about it.

And you asked, why would I want to live again, only to die again, to be locked on that trail, forever. I had stared into that locket, mesmerized by its gaze, and as I died, I saw myself die, and I knew then that we were just spirits in bodies, that we were merely floating until we faded away. I became locked in that mirror, and the person who locked me there was you.

I opened my mouth to speak, but I had no words, because I couldn't hear you but I could see through you.

I was walking toward you, catching purchase on the effervescent floor. I was going to tell you to come with me, Macy, that you did not have to become something else, this Bloody Mary, just like Dianne, when she became someone else, within the mirror. But as I walked toward you, you started shifting.

~ ~ ~

Suddenly, in the mirror, you started aging, your face shining brilliantly, like the stars, your life flashing before my eyes, until that light morphed into something much worse. The blood, a fount of crimson, rushed through your varicose veins, bursting through your bulging eyes, gasping for air.

You had become something else, Macy. Just like Dianne. The Macy I had come to know, from above, here, watching through the shadows, below, through your memories, started burning.

The scent of smoking flesh rushed through the air. The ground beneath me transformed into a bottomless pit of fire. Bloodstained fingerprints manifested in the void like gentle frost.

I reached out into the horizon, but you were melting, screaming, banshee cries echoing through the endless nothing. Blood spewed forth from your eyes in rivers, like stigmata, your reflections growing exponentially until you towered over me.

But it was no longer you.

CHAPTER THIRTY-FOUR

ERICA

Bloody Mary burst through the computer screen, neuroflashing through the mirror head-first like a newborn demon thirsting on its own blood.

Her tongue pulsed in the air, calculating the temperature of the room, the density of the sky. She flashed her predatory smile like a scar, the dead starlight shining from within.

Her shadow hands tore through the pixels and clawed at the corners of the computer monitor, grasping at the world beyond. She pushed herself through, her body elongating behind her with the infinite power of the dead starlight.

"Erica…"

Dianne seemed to look straight through her, half aware of a presence, shivering in a rush of coldness.

Bloody Mary locked eyes with me. I could feel her pulling me there, the weight of the nothingness in her blank eyes, the infinite reflection of emptiness dragging me through to the other side of the universe.

"Erica… I have traveled through your mirror, and now, you must travel through mine."

"Go away go away go away!"

I fell backwards into the dining room table, knocking over the wooden chairs, the potpourri tumbling over. The scent of fresh pine, burning meat, and winter frost swept through the air as I hid underneath the fortress of chairs, hiding for dear life.

"Dianne!" I tugged on her shoes, dragging her to safety. "Quick!"

As I watched helplessly, Bloody Mary fully materialized through the screen, powered by the pixels in the mirror that brought her to life. She loomed before us now, hovering in the air, a crimson ectoplasm dripping from her body as she slowly craned her neck toward us.

"Dianne," I whispered. "Do you see her?"

But Dianne only stared back at me, wiggling her brows playfully in quick succession just as she always had when she was slightly annoyed. She didn't know that I was trying to save her, as I had many times before. She was completely unaware of the monster that had fallen through to the other side of the mirror.

Bloody Mary floated toward the kitchen. Her crimson ectoplasm dripped onto the floor, hissing as it seeped into our carpet, burning holes through the foundation of our house like acid rain.

"On three." I pulled Dianne's arm, but she only looked at me, eyes wide. "We run to Mom and Dad's room."

"You're really scaring me, Erica."

"She's here."

"Bloody Mary?" she asked. I nodded. "Ooh, cool, what does she look like? Is she a ghost or something?"

In the kitchen, I could hear the slamming of cupboards opening and closing.

"Girls, what are you doing?" Mom called from upstairs. "It's two o'clock in the morning."

"Erica, seriously, you gotta stop whatever it is that you're doing." Dianne crawled out from underneath the table and headed toward the stairs. "Everything's fine, Mom. We just had a little too much chocolate milk."

But it was too late. Bloody Mary was charging forward, dashing through the air, the ectoplasm churning in her wake.

"Maybe it's time for both of you to go to bed," Mom said as Bloody Mary floated past me.

"Thanks for nothing, Erica," Dianne said, sighing. "Okay, Mom. Be right up."

I bolted from the table and ran toward the staircase.

I gasped. Bloody Mary was halfway up the stairs, chasing Dianne, her hands elongated into tendrils of scarlet ectoplasm. Her arms were like volcanoes dribbling lava, fossilizing into new islands, submerging anything in her path.

Dianne was nearly at the top now, inches away.

"Dianne!"

She turned around, staring right into Bloody Mary's eyes.

She froze.

Ectoplasm fell onto us like a dark fog, covering everything in sight. I ran for Dianne, shouting, crying her name, but the staircase went on and on and on.

Soon, the staircase stretched before me hundreds of miles deep.

There, at the other end of the infinite stairs, through Bloody Mary's shadow, Dianne morphed before my eyes.

"Erica, please help me." It was Dianne's voice, but as she spoke, her voice became distorted through Bloody Mary. It was the dead starlight speaking now, her voice channeling through an infinite chamber of reverb, surrounding me. "I'm scared. Help me. I'm trapped. I need to get help."

Bloody Mary reached for Dianne's braces and ripped them off, the cement that glued the metal to her teeth dissolving in Bloody Mary's touch. Dianne screamed as she clasped at her gums, her teeth rolling one by one down the stairs.

I ran after Dianne, jumping two stairs at a time, but the staircase only grew larger. Now, at the end, Dianne was eighteen, her teeth shining behind a cloud of black smoke, a cigarette hanging out of the corner of her mouth, ripping up a lotto ticket.

"Dianne!"

"Help me, Erica. But you have helped me. I'm dead, aren't I? I'm going to die soon. I don't want to die if that means I can't see you."

Bloody Mary pulled Dianne's hair and threw her down into the endless darkness, where she fell and landed two miles below on the stairs, her bones breaking and rebuilding as she became thirty, her eyes bloodshot, her varicose veins leaping out of her arms. Needles stuck out of every inch of her body, and her gums dripped with froth as she fell into her drug-induced high.

"Erica," Dianne said, slurring, but it was no longer her. She had become someone else, a mere shadow in Bloody Mary's ectoplasm. "Please. I didn't mean for it to get like this. I need help. I want to live. Help me. Please. I don't want to die."

"Just focus on my voice," I said. "I'm here for you, always."

Bloody Mary laughed as the staircase ascended into the darkness. "Go on, keep searching for it. The light."

I ran through the darkness, searching for Dianne, my mind eclipsed in a neuroflash, dragged by Bloody Mary into the place in space where memories go to die.

CHAPTER THIRTY-FIVE

I reached the top of the infinite staircase, to the place of nothingness. Above me, infinity twirled in kaleidoscopic whirls, the memories of dead starlight reflecting in such intensity I had to close my eyes to pull myself away from the gravity of their shadows.

I felt the shock of the very moment when Macy first saw herself within the mirror, when she was burning, millenniums ago, when she had died thousand upon thousands of times over, locked within the realm of her memories, in that trail, the trail that led to nothing.

Her emotions reflected into my heart, and I felt the weight of the sorrow she had bottled up, until I felt I would burst myself. My skin broke out into goosebumps, and my heart became arrhythmic, a sheer terror spreading through my chest, my eyes bulging for context, my brain melting into a neuroflash, a flash so bright it could have created the universe, these memories of it, somewhere far away.

I screamed as this monster flew through me, its shadow claws tearing through the ice mirror of my heart, its forked tongue slithering like lightning, tasting the quality of the air, feeding upon the memories that had once existed between me and Dianne.

She grew exponentially larger, folding within herself, until her shadows morphed into ectoplasm like the Northern Lights, trickling through the sky, dancing upon the planets, constellating a grandiose warmth with her fingertips.

For a moment it was almost beautiful. I had forgotten about the creature Macy had become, the monster she had called forth from the heavens, and she was something new, a star reborn, its light breathing new life into those who were lucky enough to fall into their sight.

"You have spoken my name," said Bloody Mary, her voice like crystals beneath a light rain, icicle tones resonating throughout the sky. "Tell me, what do you wish to see?"

"I want my sister to be at peace. I want Macy Abigayle to come back."

Her eyes widened, those windows to her soul shining through mine.

"I cannot do that. They are both already dead."

"No. She's here. In my heart. I just heard her. Dianne was right there, next to me, at the other end of the mirror, on top of the stairs. Macy was there, too, at the other end of the trail. We were just there, together."

"Is that so?" She frowned. "I am afraid that once you die, your memories will fade away. I cannot bring back the dead without a price."

"Then I will do anything. Please." Because although I was afraid of what she had become, this distorted reflection, I still knew that deep down, somewhere in her heart, those memories would help pull her from sinking further. "Tell me what you need, Macy. It's me."

"Macy?"

She shook your head, and a smile opened up like a scar on her face. Her lips had grown so large they tore open her flesh and the ectoplasm stopped shining; it fossilized into the shadows, and the shadows broke open with this light. It was the dead starlight I had seen with Dianne, waiting at the other end of the galaxy, and the starlight morphed into crimson, and she became an endless pool of walking blood.

She hovered toward me, slowly, gliding across the frosty, glassy surface, leaving blood in her wake like stardust, frothing at the lips.

My heart sank. Her eyes, those dark, empty cesspools of wickedness, locked into mine, and I saw myself there, infinitely reflected into the nothingness. And in that reflection, behind me, in front of me, simultaneously, she lifted her bloody hands into the air, casting a spell into the void, ectoplasm expelling from her mangled fingertips.

Behind her, all of the corpses she had risen, those foul creatures with eyes that shone with grief and loneliness, turned toward me, scanning me, eyes locked, spirits frozen, eyes wide and aglow with the dead light of the infinitely deceased stars.

"Let her go." I was losing breath as the mirror rained from the sky, crystallizing into snowflakes. The storm of Bloody Mary's voice booming in the skies shattered these fractals in a geometric snowstorm. "Please. She's everything to me."

I tried channeling the ectoplasm through my hands, but the light had already faded. I was defenseless, and Macy—Bloody Mary—knew it. What did I need to do to remember the light? What did I need to do to go on?

Bloody Mary furrowed her bloody brows and glided forward, darting between reflections, morphing into jester faces through the light, the neuroflashes in my skin jolting through my veins.

"You have called my name. I have arrived in your mirror, and now you ask me to send you back?"

She laughed, the corpses around her joining in devastating harmony. "I too thought that the stars were shining for me, girl. But the truth is, the stars do not even know you exist. They are already dead. Therefore, if you wish to see her again, you must pay with your memories, with your blood."

I nodded. "I have seen my life flash before my eyes, Bloody Mary, and now I am your reflection. Take my place here, in this world, instead."

"Give me your memories, and I will go." She reached for me, grasping for my heart. But she could not take it. It was a fortress built of memories so strong not even the Devil herself could break through. "Strange. Then I will find another way. Tell me, Erica, at the other end of this trail, what will you see?"

"I'll see a second chance." I reached for the necklace swinging from her like a pendulum. "I'll see a life ahead of me, despite what is happening around me. I'll see a new light, within reach."

"Liar." She snarled. "There is nothing on the other side of my mirror."

"Even if there is nothing there, I will find a reason to keep going."

Her hands elongated into rivers of crimson memories. She cried out, gurgling in the bloodcurdling orchestra of her gore, and through the waterfall of blood I saw her crying bloody tears, screaming as I reached through the bloodshed, to the other side of her mirror, beyond.

"No." The corpses around her lost their life. They started shrinking, falling back into infinity. "Give that back."

I opened her locket. But now it had morphed into her heart. It was a cesspool of dead memories, a void of infinite dead starlight.

She hovered over me. I was nearly drowning in blood.

"Tell me, what do you see in there, in my heart, in my home? Who will I become?" I was swimming in a sea of blood, capsizing in her tide. "You must come back and tell me," she insisted. "You must tell me!"

But I never did, and I never would, because, as I felt myself neuroflashing again, my body breaking out of the mirror like a chrysalis, ready to soar, I knew I had been here before.

As I sank further through the tide, I held my breath, prepared to face whatever waited for me on the other side.

CHAPTER THIRTY-SIX

Through the mirror, I saw two faces staring back.

They did not know it then, but they were peering into the void, a realm away, far too young to comprehend the weight of their futures. They were not prepared for their life to flash before their eyes, but it did. As they recognized their own reflections, they saw who they wanted to be, who they wanted to become.

They would not let their fears define them.

I will not let my fears define me, Bloody Mary.

I had already seen my life flash before my eyes. And through the glassy frost, I saw Dianne, peering into the void.

I melted through the computer screen, neuroflashing forward into the past.

The ectoplasm settled around my skin as I sat in the chair.

We were right there, Dianne and I, staring death straight in the face, though at the time, we were too young to know it. That's what hindsight does. It provides a kind of superpower.

Macy was there with us, too, stuck in infinity, but in that moment, as I neuroflashed to the past, I was unaware of her presence. But she was always there, all along, our guardian angel, our phantom circuit that linked us together, two trails of memories that functioned within themselves, hardwired together by those memories she had provided us all along.

She had shown us what death could be, but she also showed us how beautiful life was, too.

"Mirror, mirror, on the wall," Dianne said, "who's the fairest of them all?"

Dianne and I were sitting in front of the computer monitor. It was dark and we had already been playing video games on the computer all night. We drank a lot of chocolate milk and each had a sugar rush. We had leveled up our game playing to none other than one of the most frightening games of all.

Bloody Mary.

The memory of this moment became clearer to me as I sat there, before the mirror, the portal to Bloody Mary's realm. Possessed with the knowledge of hindsight, the significance of this moment became clearer than ever. This game had been a turning point in our childhood, when we had gained the courage to face our fears head on.

I laughed as Dianne made funny faces in the screen. She was wearing her Hello Kitty pajamas that Mom had gotten her for Christmas just days ago. We were having one of our sleepovers where we slept downstairs and watched cartoons until the early morning. Those nights were special. We would build forts out of plastic computer chairs and play video games until past midnight.

"I'm pretty fair, all right." I smiled and spit out a silly raspberry at Dianne's reflection. "I love going to the fair. Is this game fair?"

"You're so punny, Erica. Such a stinker." In the screen, she looked leagues taller than me, but really, she was just a *little* taller than me. She seemed so much older back then. Two years were two lifetimes. "That's not how the game goes, though. We don't just look into the mirror, or, I mean, the screen, and think about what her reflection looks like. If you want to conjure up her spirit, you gotta play by the rules."

"And how do *you* know all of the rules? I thought you never played this game before."

"Easy. I saw it on TV once. All you gotta do is think of what she looks like. You gotta really think of all the bad monsters you've ever seen in movies, and then imagine what all of those combined would look like. Okay, I might be stretching it now, ha, I'll admit, but at least that's how we'll play it." She laughed and then added, "Oh, yeah. One more thing. We gotta say her name three times. Misses Mary of thy Blood. I can't say it yet, because then we would already be saying it once."

"Why do you wanna play?"

"Because I just have to know who I see in the mirror. Duh. And you're not supposed to play it alone. Everyone knows how to play. It's like Duck Duck Goose, or Ring Around the Rosie. Except, *lol*, maybe it's just a little bit scarier, although Ring Around the Rosie is pretty scary, if you think about it, too. People were putting roses around their noses because of all the dead bodies back then."

I bit my lip. "I'm a little scared, Dianne. I don't know if I want to play."

"It's not any scarier than playing that game on the computer where you just keep clicking and clicking and hope you don't die. And then, if you do die, you just go back to the start, and then you keep going until you die again."

"But what if this isn't a game, Dianne? What if when we say her name, we can't restart, and we get pulled into the mirror?"

Dianne opened her mouth to speak but hesitated. She shook her head instead.

"It's just a game, Erica. Everyone knows that."

I thought of Macy, then, but my former self couldn't express just why this struck me as terrifying. I saw the expression on my face in the screen, and it made me wonder if I had known, back then, that I would be back within this moment, now, reliving the terrors that waited on the other side of the mirror, possessed with the knowledge that had haunted me for many years.

"There were real people who died there, on the Oregon Trail," I said. "They died of starvation. They died because of the snow. Some of them even turned into carnivores."

"You mean cannibals?"

"Oh. Yeah. Right. Same thing, kind of. But then someone made a game out of those people dying. And then those video game people were actually dying, again and again, stuck in a loop, forever. Kind of like when we think of bad things and then can't stop thinking of them. Isn't that a little weird, if you think about it? I mean, what if we're like those video game people, stuck, dying in the same ways, until we can't take it anymore and wish upon a star that we could get out?"

"Come on, Erica." Dianne frowned. "You're really being weird right now. I've never heard you talk like this. What makes you say that?"

For a moment, time slowed as I saw myself smile within the mirror. The world shifted a little, and I felt the ectoplasm warming throughout my veins. I must have known, back then, but I presently didn't know why.

"What if we're here, now, but our reflections are trapped in the mirror forever, and then, one day, when we learn how to relive this moment, they will break out again?"

She laughed. "Can you please just stop with your philosophical reflections? Let's just play it already."

"Okay. Whatever you say."

She turned off the living room light. My eyes readjusted to the darkness. "All right. So, you just look into the mirror, and then you say her name three times."

Something in the air shifted. I thought I saw the outline of Macy in the mirror, waiting for us, but when I blinked, I only saw my own reflection staring back.

I had become her reflection, then. It had worked. I had taken her place, and Dianne would be okay.

"Bloody Mary—"

"Wait. Dianne. What if I told you that right now…right now, this very moment, is the last moment we'll have like this, together?"

"Why are you talking like that?" Her tone was filled with fear and curiosity. "Like you know something I don't?"

"Because what if, when we look in the mirror, it's not us standing there. What if there's actually someone, or something else, staring back?"

I heard myself say these words out loud as if they were coming from someone else. Maybe it was the reflection of myself who had already fallen in the mirror.

"That wouldn't happen. Ever. It's just a game."

"You don't know that. You've never played it before."

"If it was real, then everyone who ever played it would be dead."

"But what if this time, it's different?"

"Well, my little Er-Bear, I guess there's only one way to find out." There was a sudden awareness in her voice. It was almost as if her spirit knew what was coming next, but she couldn't stop herself from saying the words we had spoken years ago. "Bloody Mary—"

"Wait!"

"Jeez-louise. What is it this time?"

"What if I told you that when we summon her, that you would be gone?" I was blinking back tears now. I did not remember this in my memories, and yet, Dianne and I both knew this was a new moment being experienced in our past. I saw the outline of her face staring at me in the mirror. It was her but not her. She was a phantom of herself, a distorted reflection of the past, waiting to break free into the distant future. "What if this is the last time I'll see you, ever again?"

Dianne furrowed her brows. "Erica, please, stop it. You're scaring me. You're giving me déjà vu. What's happening?"

"I think I know." I stepped closer to the other side that waited beyond. "The mirror holds our memories, and when you finally face them, you won't be afraid anymore. Let's say it together, then."

"I don't know if I want to play this game now, Erica."

"It's too late." I took a deep breath. "We have to. There's no choice."

She frowned, then nodded.

"Okay. Here goes."

We repeated her name one last time, the only way we could—together, linked by the invisible forces that surrounded us, always.

EPILOGUE

ERICA WESTFIELD: STATUS UPDATE

Hi everyone. I appreciate you all checking in with me. If I have left you on **READ**, please know that I have read your messages and I will get back to you sometime in the future. I might even post on my blog soon. Right now, I'm simply just overwhelmed with the outpouring of love and support you all have shown me. You have no idea what it means to me.

I wanted to share something.

I've been doing a lot of reflecting lately. I've been thinking about a lot of things, but I keep coming back to one thing.

There is a special place in my heart, one that I didn't quite know existed until recently. If home is where the heart is, then within my heart, there is something like a home, also. It is a collection of moments, memories, and experiences I have shared with loved ones, a reflection of who I was, who I know myself to be, and who I have yet to become.

It is the very place that defines me.

It is a home for Dianne, tender, forgiving, and sweet. It is a redeeming place, one that can only be created if we seek to understand what lies beyond the surface. It acts as a mirror, reminding us of our potential, guiding us through the darkness, grounding us when we have lost hope. If we have the power to understand that place, then we can share kindness to others, and, ultimately, we will have the power to change the future.

Right now, we are alive, a miracle that only lasts a lifetime. If my home is fueled by the people who live there, by all of you, then deep within my soul, this home will live on, for as long as I am alive, for as long as I remember.

I do not wish to know what death after death is like, if there is an end to the end. No one really knows. I don't know what happens when these memories fade away.

Even if everything surrounding my reflection transforms completely, these memories are the moments that have helped shape me. I would not know who I am if I did not have this place, this mirror, if I did not think of all of the joy and wonder that my heart contains.

No matter what may happen after life, the memory of this love will be there, too, because I have seen it pull me through the shadows.

I do not know when I will really see Dianne again.

But when I start to feel myself sinking again, I just think of this place in my heart.

And I remember these memories that are with me, always.

And I get a feeling, like I am alive.

~ THE END

ACKNOWLEDGEMENTS

Thank you to everyone who has supported me on my writing journey. I've spent many years typing away on my laptop in coffeeshops and libraries learning the craft of writing, and I couldn't have done any of this without your help.

Thank you, Mom and Dad, for supporting me unconditionally throughout every aspect of my life. Thank you for helping me on my journey through the arts. I couldn't have done any of this without your love and support, which will always be an understatement.

Thanks to my brothers, Addam and Heath, for all of your encouragement. Thanks for letting me tell you all of my story ideas ever since I called myself a writer (and for letting me ramble on about these stories, especially before playing shows). I'm grateful to create music and art with you. Thanks to my sisters-in-law, Mia and Jessica, for all that you do. I'm really grateful to call you family. Thanks to all my extended family for your support. Thanks to Grandma Sandy, Aunt Robin, and Lark and Tony Anctil for reading some of the earliest drafts of my stories.

I want to say a huge thanks to my editor, Stephanie Slagle, for your invaluable feedback during edits. This novel is so much stronger because of your knowledge in storytelling. I sincerely appreciate your time on this story and your expertise in the craft of writing and editing. Thank you very much.

There are many incredible resources available for emerging writers. I want to say a huge thanks to the authors who have given their time and energy back to these writing communities. A very special thanks Jonathan Maberry and the Writers Coffeehouse, Scott Sigler, Henry Herz, Peter Clines, Christoph Paul, Susan Dennard and the Mighty Pens, Chris Ryall, Michael A. Ventrella, R. J. Crowther Jr., and Jon Cooksey.

Thank you to authors Dennis Crosby, Indy Quillen, J. Dianne Dotson, Leighton Reynolds, Amanda Matula, Lindsay Lerman, Luke Tarzian, Autumn Christian, Lizz Huerta, Ruby Mellinger, Chad Stroup, Renee Pickup, Tanya Rochester, Tone Milazzo, Ben Spada, Dr. Janina Scarlet, Elle Jauffret, Gordon Dunleavy, Dr. Billy Sense, Jason Whitfield, Tori Eldridge, The Winner Twins, and Mya Duong.

I couldn't have developed as a writer if I didn't have access to the incredible resources available through Mysterious Galaxy Bookstore. A huge thanks to all of the amazing booksellers for their hard work. Thanks for creating one of the most incredible creative scenes out there. I have learned so much by talking to you all and by attending these author events, writer groups, and more. Thank you.

Thanks to all of my friends and mentors who have helped me along the way, as well as my friends I have been fortunate enough to work alongside with in the arts while creating this novel. Thanks to Chase Ryan, Theo Iyer, Arya Zarifi, Brantzen Wong, Steven Polc, Lyndon Pugeda, Mona Sleiman, Tiffanie Dang, Dee Jaye Jackson, Lisa Hiser, Cody Boukather, Chelsea Holmes, Westin Mills, Daniel Catullo, Bruce Mohler, Dave Smith, Blake Gould, Brian Klemm, Vincent Walker, Tyler Davis, Greg Parker, Zach Halop, Tony Duran, Luke Lucas, Seve Wada, Tolan Shaw, John Hartmann, Guy Eckstine, Dahni Shaw, Rohan Ramanan, Teneyah Olmstead, Jackie Luna, Casey Purvis, Pamela Raber, June Selbo, Scott Brazee, Jack Wagner, Steve Smith, Dave Malmgren, Daniel Filippi, Trevor Wright, Beto Suarez, Pitch Michael, and Tyler Phillips. Thank you to the authors featured on The Bookshelf Symphony Orchestra. A very special thanks to Ryan Kilpatrick and Matthew Champagne.

ABOUT THE AUTHOR

Austin Farmer is a musician, author, and filmmaker from Southern California. During his early high school years, Austin recorded with his band The Bolts in Capitol Records Studio B alongside the late Producer Andy Johns (The Rolling Stones, Led Zeppelin).

His songs with The Bolts and Island Apollo have landed music licensing spots on MLB, NASCAR, Fox Sports, Nickelodeon, and more. Most recently, his production music created with brothers Addam and Heath Farmer can be heard in the video game MLB The Show 2021. Austin served as the Director of Music and Music Supervisor for multiple music libraries. He currently plays in bands Nada Robot, Island Apollo, and Superweapon, as well as cover bands at different theme parks. He is also the singer of Anthem San Diego Rush Tribute.

His original orchestral album, The Bookshelf Symphony Orchestra, an instrumental album for readers and writers inspired by some of his favorite books, can be found on all streaming services. His short story, Beethoven's Baton, was published in Baker Street Irregulars Vol. 1 (Diversion Books, co-edited by Michael A. Ventrella and Jonathan Maberry).

For years, before shows with his bands, Austin would read and write stories while hanging out at coffee shops near venues. His coffee drink of choice is iced hazelnut coffee and his backpack is usually stuffed with too many books. He currently lives in San Diego, California.